MW00848593

"Trace Conger is establishing himself as one of the most original voices in crime fiction." - Gregory Petersen, author of *Open Mike* and *The Dream Thief*

"Trace Conger's characters are well-plumbed, original and real." - Bookpostmortem

"Conger's writing is direct. It moves clearly and quickly, perfect for thrillers." - Ronald Tierney, author of the Deets Shanahan Mysteries

"*The Prison Guard's Son* is a superbly crafted crime novel. The characters are richly drawn with a rare combination of nuance and depth... This is one of the year's best books." - Mysterious Reviews

"The Mr. Finn series breathes new life into the P.I. genre... It is one of the best detective series I've ever read." - Gumshoes, Gats and Gams

"*The Shadow Broker* tips a handsome hat in the direction of old-fashioned pulp fiction and it does so with considerable style. The writing is fluid and the plot pumps along." - Murder, Mayhem & More

TRACE CONGER

MIRAGE MAN

A CONNOR HARDING THRILLER

Mirage Man

Copyright © 2021 by Trace Conger

All rights reserved.

Without limiting the rights under copyright reserved above, no part of this publication may be reproduced, stored in or introduced into a retrieval system, or transmitted, in any form, or by any means (electronic, mechanical, photocopying, recording, or otherwise) without the prior written permission of both the copyright owner and the above publisher of this book.

This is a work of fiction. Names, characters, places, brands, media, and incidents are either the product of the author's imagination or are used fictitiously. The author acknowledges the trademarked status and trademark owners of various products, brands, bands, and/or restaurants referenced in this work of fiction, which have been used without permission. The publication/use of these trademarks is not authorized, associated with, or sponsored by the trademark owners.

Cover design by Damonza.

Interior design and formatting by the handsome devils at

Black Mill Books

ISBN: 13: 978-0-9968267-6-1

ISBN-10:-0-9968267-6-9

Printed in the United States of America

Library of Congress Cataloging-in-Publication Data

Conger, Trace

Mirage Man (A Connor Harding Novel) — 1st edition

To all of those who have supported me on this journey, I owe you more than I can ever repay.

And a special thank you to my family who continue to believe in me, even when I sometimes do not.

"There's two angels sittin on my shoulders.
All they ever do is disagree.
One sits on the side of rhyme and reason.
The other on the reckless side of me."

— "THE RECKLESS SIDE OF ME," THE
STEELDRIVERS

"Not all who wander are lost."

— J. R. R. TOLKIEN

1
DISAPPEARING ACT

PEOPLE DISAPPEAR ALL THE TIME. Sometimes, they go voluntarily, and sometimes they don't. Denise Rodriquez fell into the first category. She wanted to vanish and she wanted to take her six-year-old daughter, Lola, with her.

Mr. Fish and I were going to make that happen, we just hadn't expected to do it today.

Creating a new identity for someone, surgically plucking them out of their current existence, and then dropping them into their New World isn't some sleight of hand you conjure up over a weekend. It takes planning, and you better get it right. We're talking a new driver's license, birth certificates, Social Security numbers, bank accounts, and vehicle registrations, not to mention fabricated employment, credit and medical histories.

The toughest part was Denise's criminal record. She served six months in MCI–Framingham for drug possession and distribution, which meant her fingerprints were on file. Anyone with the right connections and bankroll can create a halfway decent identity for someone, but altering prints in the

FBI's Next Generation Identification system, the bureau's central repository of biometric info, was something else.

That's what Mr. Fish and I do. We make people disappear, and we know what we're doing. We're as good as WITSEC, but unlike the FBI, we don't require anyone to testify before they become invisible. As long as Denise doesn't slip up and out herself, she's as good as gone.

Denise could have gone to the FBI and offered up information on Ernesto "Trinidad" Rodriquez, her husband and Lola's father, in exchange for a life far away from Boston, but there was no guarantee they would play ball. By coming to us, she gets to disappear on her own terms.

Ernesto was the shot caller for the Westside Assassins, a local street gang. Denise didn't have a problem with Ernesto's violent streak when it stayed on the street, but when it crept into their home and Lola's room, she decided it was time to run.

The original plan gave us another three weeks to generate all the documents, confirm her new information was in the right databases, and pressure test her new identity under a variety of scenarios, like a traffic stop or a trip to the voting booth. But that window slammed shut the moment Ernesto found out Denise wanted to flee.

I don't know how he found out, but Denise was able to get a text message to Mr. Fish alerting him that Ernesto was onto her. Mr. Fish told her to get Lola and drive to a nearby supermarket parking lot, where we would meet her. We arrived ten minutes after Mr. Fish sent the message.

"I don't like it," I said, scanning the parking lot for Denise's BMW.

Mr. Fish tapped his index finger against the side of his

nose. "All she had to do was buy enough time to get to her car. Let's give her another fifteen. Then we'll try the house."

Fifteen minutes seemed like an hour, but when Denise still hadn't shown, Mr. Fish kicked the car into gear and drove the two miles to her house. He parked down the street.

The BMW was still in the driveway. Two other cars blocked it in. The SUV belonged to Ernesto. Who drove the black pickup truck was anyone's guess.

"At least we know she's still here," said Mr. Fish.

"Right, but is she still breathing? And who else is in there?"

We didn't have to wait long for the answer. A big guy wearing a white V-neck T-shirt and jeans came out of the house first. A smaller man, dressed the same, came out behind him. Denise followed, and then Ernesto emerged, dragging Lola by the arm. He didn't bother to hide the piece in his waistband.

They all piled into the SUV and pulled out. Mr. Fish gave them a cushion and then pulled out behind them.

Based on their route, we knew where they were headed. The Westside Assassins operated out of a housing complex called Lot 72 in Boston's Roxbury neighborhood. If Ernesto and his crew made it inside the complex, Denise was likely not walking back out.

We tailed them for several miles, waiting for an opportunity to intercept them. Finally, they pulled off the main highway onto a less populated two-lane road. Strip malls boasting everything from coffee shops to gas stations to fast-food restaurants littered both sides of the street.

"We need them to pull over," I said.

"How do you suppose we get them to do that?"

"Get closer, but stay on the passenger side on the car."

Mr. Fish closed the gap as I pulled out my .45 and screwed on the suppressor.

"You're going to start a shoot-out on the highway? Not smart."

"Not a shoot-out," I said. "Hang back a bit and try to get in his blind spot."

As Mr. Fish jockeyed into position, I crawled into the back seat and rolled down the rear window on the driver's side. Then I buried a slug in the SUV's rear passenger tire. From a distance, an accurate shot might not even break through a steel-belted radial, but we were close enough to do some damage.

Contrary to popular belief, tires don't explode when shot. They puncture, producing a slow bleed like running over a nail. The driver wouldn't even know anything had happened until the tire flattened out, then he'd have to pull off the road and change it. Even if Ernesto inspected the busted radial, it would be too flat to spot a bullet hole.

With a .45-caliber hole in it, the tire deflated in less than a minute. The driver immediately slowed and eased over into the right lane. We passed them so they wouldn't make the tail. Mr. Fish took the next turnoff into a clothing store parking lot and doubled back, where we found Ernesto's SUV sitting lopsided at a gas station.

Mr. Fish cut the engine. "Now what?"

The bigger man in the white T-shirt opened the liftgate and removed a tire iron and jack.

"We've got to separate Denise and Lola from Ernesto's crew," I said. "And we need to do it fast before they change that tire."

4

Mr. Fish grabbed his phone from the console and opened Denise's last text message. He replied, instructing her to take Lola inside the store. "I hope Ernesto didn't confiscate her phone," he said.

A minute later, Denise and Lola emerged from the SUV and walked toward the King Kwik convenience store. Ernesto followed.

I removed the suppressor, slipped the .45 into my jacket pocket, and stepped out of the car. A rush of adrenaline surged through me, and I felt my heart hammering inside my chest. It had been a while since I felt that.

"Pull around back and keep the engine running," I said.

Mr. Fish said something, but I was already too far away to make it out. I entered the convenience store and walked toward the back. The sixty-something-year-old cashier stood behind a two-inch-thick Plexiglas window. There were three security cameras positioned near the ceiling, covering the entire store. No blind spots.

I passed a rubber door with a plastic window that led to a back room. Next to that was a small recessed hallway, where Ernesto stood outside the bathroom door. Denise and Lola must be inside. The toilet flushed, so I moved around a shelf of candy bars and automotive magazines with my back to Ernesto. The door opened and Denise and Lola came out. Ernesto followed on their heels.

Once he passed me, I turned and wrapped my forearm around his neck and squeezed. Rendering someone unconscious by compressing both carotid arteries takes less than six seconds. It also only takes as much pressure as opening a can of Diet Coke. Once someone gets a solid grip on you, there isn't much you can do to stay on your feet. When Ernesto went limp, I laid him down on the filthy blue-and-white tile floor and released the hold.

"Out the back," I said. "Let's go!"

It took Denise a moment to recognize me before she grabbed Lola by the hand. They followed me through the rubber door next to the bathroom, through a small stockroom, and out a brown dented metal door that led to the rear parking lot, where Mr. Fish waited in his humming sedan.

Ernesto would regain consciousness within sixty seconds, but he'd have no idea why he was on the floor, a side effect caused by the momentary lack of oxygen to his brain. The four of us would be long gone by the time he made it back to his boys playing mechanic and figured out what had just happened.

WE ARRIVED at a safe house in Worcester, Massachusetts, about an hour later. Denise and Lola would stay there until we had all the documents they needed to start over. In a few weeks, Mr. Fish would drive back to Worcester and deliver their paperwork, then take them to Bradley International Airport, where they would board a flight to Somewhere, USA, and put Ernesto's heavy hand behind them forever.

2

OLD HABITS

MR. FISH WAS one of the first people I met when I moved to Boston two years ago. I had rented an apartment until I could find a house, and after unpacking for several hours, I made my way to a nearby watering hole. Less than a minute after I sat down at the bar, a pudgy man wearing suspenders—the only person I'd seen in suspenders in a decade or more—sidled up next to me and asked what I was drinking.

I told him Dewar's and he walked behind the bar and poured me two fingers of scotch liked he owned the place. I'd later find out he didn't own it, he just knew the owner well enough to have behind-the-bar privileges.

Mr. Fish was an ex-cop turned PI. He used to work the typical PI cases, but then he carved out a niche selling new identities to anyone who could afford the twenty-grand price tag. Sometimes, he did pro bono work for those like Denise who couldn't afford the cost of a new life, but who, according to Mr. Fish, deserved one.

He was in his early sixties, short, balding, unassuming, and his suits never seemed to fit right. What he lacked in fashion sense, he made up for with a wicked sense of humor and familiarity with half the city of Boston. He knew everyone worth knowing. Those connections made him a damn good PI and gave him access to everything he needed to build new identities from scratch. He once told me all he needed to locate someone or help someone vanish was a fully charged cell phone and a comfortable couch.

WE WERE twenty minutes into the car ride back to Boston when Mr. Fish turned and stared at me. It was the kind of look you didn't need to see. You felt it, like a grease burn. I glanced over, expecting him to say something and then turn back toward the highway in front of us, but he didn't. He just kept glaring at me.

"You might want to keep those eyes on the road," I said.

"How long have we been working together?"

"What, maybe eighteen months?"

He continued to stare.

"The road," I said.

He returned his eyes to the asphalt and readjusted his grip on the steering wheel. "Eighteen months and you never pulled something like that."

"You know as well as I do if Ernesto got her to that complex she was done. We didn't have time to run a plan through committee."

"For the most part, you're a smart kid. But you're capable of some stupid shit. I figure you noticed the four cameras outside the store? I assume there were at least two inside."

"Three."

"And how long do you think it's going to take Ernesto to get ahold of that footage and identify you?"

"He's a street thug—"

"And then connect you to me," he interrupted.

"Ernesto doesn't have the connections to ID me. And even if he did, I'd never lead him to you."

Mr. Fish smirked behind the wheel. "What about my plates? Maybe they're able to pick them up from the video feed. I'm sure they've got a nice clean shot of you getting out of the car and walking inside the store."

"I didn't beat down some nun on the street, Fish."

"No, you beat down the shot caller for a brutal street gang."

"Small-time thug. Nobody outside his gang gives two shits what happens to him. No cop is going to spend his overtime running down leads. I wouldn't worry about it."

"That's the thing. You don't worry about it. You don't worry about anything. And you should. You assaulted someone in broad daylight, on camera. Even if Boston PD doesn't pursue it, it won't take much for Ernesto to find out who you are. You've compromised our operation, and you've put me at risk."

"Fish, I didn't—"

"Bullshit. There's no way Ernesto lets this go. Not with his wife and daughter gone. I guarantee he, or someone he works with, has connections with the PD. I bet he has your name and address, or worse, mine, in forty-eight hours."

"If he comes knocking, I'll handle it. Ernesto Rodriquez isn't the scariest person in this town."

"No. No, he's not."

He was right to be concerned. Mr. Fish was as cautious as

they come. Given what he does for a living, he has to be. Of all the adjectives to describe me though, "cautious" might not be on the list. And if it was, it'd be way down near the bottom.

We didn't speak again until he stopped in front of my home.

"One of these days, your past is gonna come knocking, kid. Keep a level head next time. I don't like working with gunslingers. They tend to get dead."

"I'll take care of it," I said, getting out of the car. "Ernesto won't be an issue."

He looked at me with an expression that was impossible to read.

"See that you do," he finally said before driving off.

3

GOOD NEWS AND BAD ANALOGIES

I WALKED into the house to find my father, Albert, sitting on the couch. He had a Lawrence Block novel in one hand and a glass of whiskey in the other. The bottle was on the coffee table in front of him. Albert had completed his last round of chemotherapy for stage-three prostate cancer six months ago, and he'd had a follow-up appointment with his oncologist this morning to review his latest test results. I couldn't tell if the bottle meant he was celebrating or drinking away bad news.

He looked up at me but didn't tip his hand.

"So? What the doctor say?"

Albert closed the novel, yanked the cork from the bottle, and refreshed his glass.

"Cancer-free, bitch."

A calm washed over me, and for a moment, I forgot all about Ernesto, Mr. Fish, and everything else.

"That's great news. We should go out and celebrate."

He swirled the glass in his hand. "Already started."

I grabbed a glass and sat down next to him.

"That's really great news," I said. "It's exactly what I needed to hear today."

"Well, don't go getting sentimental on me. Just know I won't be haunting you for a bit longer."

"I'll take it."

I tried to get my father up and out of the house, but he wanted to stay in and read his novel. We polished off a pizza and I settled into my own book.

An hour later, he closed the Block novel and tossed it onto the coffee table.

"Oh," he said. "I need you to take me to the bus station."

"What?"

"I'm going to Cincinnati to see your brother and I need you to take me to the bus station."

"When did you decide to go to Cincinnati?"

"About ten minutes before I bought the ticket. Want to tell him the good news in person."

A trip to Cincinnati was precisely what Albert needed. Finn and his family wouldn't let him sit inside, eat pizza, and read pulp paperbacks. They'd fawn over him in a way that wasn't in me.

"When are you going?"

He looked at his watch. "In a few hours."

"Thanks for the notice."

"Small price to pay to get rid of me for a week."

Albert didn't fly. It's not that he was afraid to fly, rather, he preferred to inconvenience me with a trip to the bus station at three in the morning, which seems to be the only time busses leave Boston.

"What time?"

"Bus leaves at six-forty in the morning."

"Well, that's not as annoying as your typical schedule."

"You got off easy this time. Finn has to pick me up at four forty-five in the morning."

"Glad he doesn't get to sleep in either."

As much as I wasn't looking forward to whisking my father to the Boston bus terminal before the sun came up, I was glad he would be out of town for a while. That would give me time to handle any trouble Ernesto created for me without worrying about Albert's safety.

THE NEXT MORNING, we were on the road by five. Albert wanted to leave early to beat the nonexistent Saturday rush hour traffic.

My father was the observant type and could tell a lot about a man just by looking at him. He sensed something was bothering me and demanded to know what it was. Perhaps he wanted a clear conscience before he left for Cincinnati.

I told him about the encounter with Ernesto, and he said I did the right thing given the circumstances.

"But Fish is right about something too," he said. "You're an idiot if you're not at least a little concerned about this Ernesto person. Even if *he* gives up on finding you, there's always someone else who's going to be waiting in the wings. Ready to stomp you out for something you did who knows when. I'd rather see you in some safe career—running a business, sitting at a desk or something. You always were a smart kid. Much smarter than your brother. I figured you'd be the one who went off and did something big."

"You mean boring and predictable? Sorry to disappoint you."

"You know what I mean, Connor. The problem with your lifestyle is the cumulative amount of blowback following you around." He thought for a moment. "Your life is like walking around with dog turds in your pocket."

"What the hell are you talking about?"

"I'm talking about you. You walk through life associating with bad people, and those people have a collective effect on your life."

"And this relates to dog crap how?"

"It's an analogy, try to keep up. The dog turds represent all the toxic people you associate with. Those morons you got mixed up with in the army and all that crap in New York. Every time you're with those people, it's like sticking a turd in your pocket. After a while, you start to stink.

"Then, one day, you decide you've had enough of working with miscreants, so you cut them out of your life. And you dump all those turds out of your pocket. You're done with them. But guess what? Even though you unload all the crap you've been carrying around with you, you still stink. You can't wash that off."

"Dad, that's the worst analogy I've ever heard. Ever."

"You know what I mean."

"Why wouldn't I just buy another coat? One that doesn't smell like dog shit?"

"You can't just buy another coat, because then the analogy doesn't work. The smell follows you around forever, Connor, because you can't shake all the bad karma in your life. It catches up. Sticks to ya."

My father tried his best to deliver on that teachable moment, but like many things, he did it in his own unique way.

When we arrived at the bus terminal, I got him to his gate and left him with his suitcase and a hot cup of coffee. I offered to stay until he boarded the bus, but he brushed me off and told me to get on with my weekend.

"I'll be back next Saturday," he said. "Pick me up at six o'clock."

I didn't have to ask if it was a.m. or p.m.

Albert began chatting up the attractive terminal attendant as I slipped away.

I WAS WALKING into my house when Mr. Fish rang me.

"Tell me you had nothing to do with this," he said.

"Unless Albert burned down the Boston Port Authority, I'm completely in the clear."

"I'm serious."

"And I seriously don't know what you're talking about."

"They pulled Ernesto Rodriquez out of a ditch this morning. Someone put two holes in his head and dumped him a mile from his house."

"No shit?"

"And you don't know anything about it?"

"No, I don't. I was with Albert last night. And this morning. Can't be two places at once."

"Maybe you called it in. Had someone else do it for you."

"No. I take care of my own messes. I'm clean on this, Fish. I had nothing to do with it."

"I didn't really think you did, but I had to ask. I don't know how much effort Boston PD is going to put into investigating this, but if they ID you in the surveillance video, they might come asking questions."

"Let 'em ask. I've got nothing to do with it."

"I guess you can sleep a little easier now," said Mr. Fish.

"Guess so. Keep me posted if you hear anything."

"I'll do that."

4

THE DEAD MAN ON THE FLOOR

IT HAD BEEN two years since someone tried to kill me.

Had the dead man on my kitchen floor known what he was doing, perhaps he'd be standing over *my* body and not the other way around. Lucky for me, he didn't know my back door squeaked like a cheap motel bed. He also forgot his safety was on. That's what saved my life.

When I surprised him in the kitchen, he tried to squeeze off a round from his 9mm, realized his mistake, and in the time it took him to glance down and disengage the safety, I'd grabbed a boning knife from the block on the counter and thrust it up through his left lung and into his heart.

I wasn't shocked Ernesto sent someone to kill me, but I was surprised he arrived so quickly. It had only been twenty-four hours since I introduced my forearm to Ernesto's carotid arteries, and I severely underestimated his ability to identify me this fast. There's no way he ran Mr. Fish's license plate or identified me from some grainy gas station surveillance video without someone from Boston PD feeding him information.

Without help, Ernesto would have been killed and stuffed in that ditch long before he connected the dots.

I stepped back to avoid the crimson blood that oozed out from underneath the body and seeped toward my feet. Dropping the long, thin knife into the sink, I realized some of the blood dripping from my right hand didn't belong to the man on the floor. It was mine. I thrust the knife into him so hard my hand slid up the handle and onto the blade, slicing my fingers open. The lacerations weren't deep, but as my adrenaline slowed, the pain surged in.

Wrapping a dish towel around the wound, I leaned against the counter, closed my eyes, and waited for my heartbeat to return to normal. After a few minutes, my hands had stopped shaking. The twitch above my left eye continued.

I rolled John Doe onto his back with my foot, kicked off his Boston Celtics cap, and knelt over him, keeping a close eye on the widening blood trail that followed me like smoke at a campfire.

I didn't recognize him. I can't say with complete certainty I'd never seen him before, but if I had, he wasn't memorable. He had buzzed dark hair, looked twenty-five to thirty years old with an athletic build, and carried a scar on his right cheek just below the eye. He didn't look like a gangbanger, but it's likely Ernesto hired someone from outside his crew. That way, there would be less chance of anyone tying the shooter back to the Westside Assassins.

The pockets of the dead man's black hoodie were empty, so I checked the matching sweatpants for a wallet or some other form of identification. All I found was a spare magazine and a scrap of paper with my name and address. The watch on his wrist was large and gaudy, with lots of diamonds. Something you wore to get noticed. I stripped it off his wrist and checked the back for an inscription. Nothing. Lifting his shirt, I checked for tattoos, anything that might have a name or gang affiliation. Nothing. I shifted my attention to his legs. Rolling up his pants legs, I found a large green shamrock on his right calf. Anywhere else in the country, that ink might be telling, but this was Boston and shamrock tattoos were as common as Catholics.

Contract killers come in a few sizes. You've got low-level street thugs, who will gun anyone down for a gram of crystal meth and pocket change. Even if they do succeed in killing a mark, they'll do something stupid and get caught within hours, probably only a few miles from the crime scene. Then you've got your career professionals. Those are the ones you never see coming. They'll learn your routine over days, if not weeks, and put a bullet in your head when you're out walking your dog some Tuesday evening after *Jeopardy*. They're precise and intelligent, which is why they don't get caught. And they know when their safety is on. The guy on my floor was somewhere in between, and I was insulted that Ernesto didn't send someone with more experience.

Or maybe he did send someone with experience, they were just waiting in a car outside. Hit squads usually work in pairs, one shooter and one driver, which meant there was a good chance number two was nearby growing more nervous by the minute.

I clicked off the kitchen light, tossed the dish towel, and picked up the 9mm. It felt cold against my throbbing hand. I slipped out the back door. The sun had set hours ago, but the streetlamps lit up the road behind my house like an airport runway at midnight. A Porsche SUV idled a block away. It didn't belong to anyone who lived on my street. I tucked the 9mm under my shirt and ran toward the vehicle, staying just outside the wash from the overhead streetlights. Without the dish towel, my fingers bled down the handle of the 9mm and onto my pants leg as I made my way toward the SUV.

I'd closed to within twenty feet of the vehicle when it squealed its tires and bolted away leaving a burnt-rubber stench lingering in the air. The driver must have noticed I wasn't his partner and assumed the hit had gone south. I caught all six digits on his Massachusetts license plate as he tore down the suburban street.

Back in my kitchen, I cleaned off my hand and dressed it with something more sterile than a dish towel. Then I snapped the dead man's photo with my cell phone. When it came to identifying the man staining my kitchen tile, Mr. Fish was my go-to call.

"It's late," he said, answering the phone without a hello. "What did you do this time?"

"There's a dead man in my kitchen."

"Did you kill him?"

"Yeah, but it was justified. He broke into my home looking to put a few holes in me."

"I told you shit was going to follow you home, Connor."

"Can the lecture."

"Is it one of Ernesto's men?"

"I assume so." Using two fingers, I slid my front curtains to the side and peered down the street. "That's why I'm calling you. If I send you his photo, do you think you can identify him?"

"Why didn't you ask his name before you killed him? That

would have made things much easier." His grin was evident through the phone.

"I didn't have time for a conversation."

Except for my neighbor from two houses down walking his cocker spaniel, the street was clear.

"I'll see what I can do," said Mr. Fish.

"You might have to get off your couch for this one."

"Doubt it. Send me the photo."

I texted Mr. Fish the photograph. While I waited for him to get the image, I moved to the kitchen, and with the lights still off, surveyed the road behind my house through the window.

"You get it?" I asked.

"I've got it."

A Chevy Tahoe with its headlights turned off crawled down the street just beyond my back yard, the same street where the Porsche had been parked earlier. I snatched the 9mm from the kitchen table, clicked on my phone's speaker and lowered it to my waist to blunt the light from the screen. The Chevy stopped behind the house next to mine, but no one got out.

"I can't be positive," said Mr. Fish, "but it looks like Lucky Walsh. He used to have longer hair. Shoulder length. Does he have a shamrock tattoo on his calf? Can't remember if it's right or left."

"Yeah, right leg."

"Then that's Lucky. Guess he didn't live up to his name."

"Guess not. Who is he?"

The Chevy's dome light clicked on, as if someone had opened the door, and then slowly dimmed.

"Last I knew, he was an associate in the O'Bannon Crew,

although by now he might be a full-fledged member. The Irish Mob doesn't put out a newsletter."

"I didn't realize the Westside Assassins were connected to the Irish Mob."

"They're not, Connor. Alfie O'Bannon would never work with Ernesto's crew. He's old school and wouldn't associate with a Latin street gang. The Irish Mob isn't an equal-opportunity employer."

"Then why in the hell is there a dead Irish mobster in my kitchen?"

"This isn't connected to Ernesto. You must have pissed off someone else. Like I said—"

"Should I be worried about this Alfie O'Bannon?"

I checked that the back door was locked and surveyed the Chevy through the window again. After a moment, it rolled slowly away, its headlights still off.

"Yeah, Connor, you should be worried. O'Bannon's a big deal around here. Used to run with Whitey Bulger and the Winter Hill Gang back in the day."

"If he's such a big shot, why haven't I heard of him?"

I ran to the front of the house and checked for anyone approaching. Aside from my neighbor picking up dog crap, it was clear.

"Keeps a low profile these days. I guess unless you're working with the Irish Mob, you've got no reason to know him. Although you'd know if you did something to make him want to pop you."

"I didn't cross anyone. But there has to be some connection. I assume the Irish Mob doesn't put out contracts without a reason. You know where I can find him?"

"Last I heard, he ran a chop shop in East Somerville. I'll

see if I can look it up and shoot you the address, but I'm not sure poking around there is a smart idea. Alfie O'Bannon might be a fossil, but he's still a dangerous man. He's the type of guy who won't think twice about sealing you up in an industrial barrel and tossing you in the bay. You might want to back off."

"I can't back off. If someone wants me dead, I want to know why."

I left the living room and took the stairs two at a time, dashed into the spare bedroom, and checked the street behind my house again from the window.

"Why don't you get out of town for a while? I can ask around, see what I can find out. Be a safer option than sticking your neck out."

"Thanks for the offer," I said. "But I'm not going to rope you into this, especially if O'Bannon is as dangerous as you say he is. The info you gave me is help enough."

"Just sit tight for a bit and—"

"Sitting tight isn't going to help. When word gets back to him, or to whoever, that Lucky wasn't so lucky, they'll send someone else. Someone better."

"What about the police? If you're clean, you've got no reason not to call 'em."

"That could cause more problems. I'll talk to O'Bannon and get to the bottom of it."

"I never pictured Alfie as the talking type, but you've got balls as big as church bells if you're looking for a sit-down with the Irish Mob."

"I've got a dead man in my kitchen, a list of questions, and nothing else to do, Fish."

"Based on our conversation yesterday, I figured you'd cool

down a bit, but I see that's not the case. I'm not going to waste my breath trying to talk you out of it because you're too stupid to listen to reason. If this goes sideways, you're going to die in there, Connor. And I'll be seeing you on the evening news."

"If this goes sideways, you'll never see me again."

I clicked off the phone and stashed it in my pocket. The Chevy hadn't returned. It could have been the teenage girl from down the street getting dropped off after curfew, or it could be a drive-by to check whether the Boston PD was camped out at my house.

The driver of the SUV would have already called his boss to tell him what happened. The boss would be thinking through his options on what to do next. They wouldn't move on me tonight because they would expect me to call the police, which meant my house would be swarming with uniformed officers, a detective or two, a medical examiner, and maybe even a reporter who had been listening to a police scanner. No thug in his right mind would risk walking into that. I didn't call the police, of course. There were other ways of handling situations like this.

I needed to get John Doe out of my kitchen and into my car before he stiffened up. If I waited too long, I wouldn't be able to bend him and would have to start cutting off body parts.

Over the next few hours, I got busy cleaning up. I folded the body in half, wrapped it in plastic, rolled it up in a blue tarp, secured it with ratchet tie downs, and stashed it in the back of my Jeep. After I packed him safely away, I cleaned up the mess on my kitchen floor using oxygen bleach—chlorine bleach won't eliminate DNA evidence—and scrubbed the boning knife so hard I nearly took off the edge.

Satisfied with the clean up, I packed a bag with a few days' worth of clothes and some other essentials. I tossed Lucky's 9mm into the bag, exchanging it for my .45 from the night-stand, slipped on my coat, and headed to the garage.

After opening the garage door, I slipped out onto my driveway and checked the side yard. It was clear. Taking a final look down the street, I was satisfied I was alone. I fired up the Jeep and backed down the driveway with the .45 in my hand.

Around one in the morning, I checked into a Holiday Inn. Lucky Walsh stayed in the Jeep.

5

MOUSETRAP

THE NEXT MORNING, I sat in the Holiday Inn polishing off a complimentary breakfast of Cap'n Crunch, yogurt, and coffee. Most people never worry about someone trying to kill them. My previous professions kept me out of that category. I have been looking over my shoulder for so long that I developed a permanent crick in my neck. After eliminating Ernesto from the list of people calling in the hit, you would think I might have a clearer idea of who wanted me dead, but that wasn't the case.

Before moving to Boston two years ago, I worked in New York for a variety of people most individuals would never want to associate with. While those relationships were good for my bank account, they clashed with my desire to live a long life, which is one of the reasons I left and moved to Boston.

I retired in the right way; I asked for a way out, and thanks to years of loyal service and a habit of keeping my mouth shut, my employer obliged. Now, I wondered if he changed his mind.

The dead man wrapped up like an early Christmas present left me three options. If I stayed in Boston, whoever was behind the assassination attempt would send someone else. That's how it worked. They already knew where I lived, so whoever came after Lucky in the hitting lineup would likely surprise Albert and me at home and dispatch us both. I was fortunate to get the drop on Lucky, but I couldn't count on fortune smiling my way twice.

My other option was to run. Mr. Fish was in that camp; my father would be too. Just go. I had the means and the money to disappear and start over somewhere else. Mr. Fish and I helped a dozen people vanish over the last eighteen months, but that wasn't a possibility for me. Those people had nothing to anchor them to their desertion points. I had Albert. My New York associates already knew about him and it wouldn't take them long to uncover my brother, his wife and daughter. If I ran, whoever wanted me dead would use my family as a bargaining chip to flush me out from hiding. If I stayed under, they'd murder everyone connected to me.

That left an offensive strategy. I had to go to them. I still had some favors I could call in, and depending on who was behind this, I might be able to negotiate a way out. But before I get to that point, I had to figure out who wanted to delete me from the historical record. But a quick trip to New York was dangerous without first learning who was calling the shots. I needed to know what I was walking into, and Alfie O'Bannon was my only lead.

The bright screen of my cell phone lit up the dim corner of the room. Mr. Fish had emailed me the name of O'Bannon's chop shop, Vic's Automotive, and a link to turn-by-turn directions. Underneath the link was a message: *I won't try to change your mind, but this is a mistake. Consequences, Connor.*

He was probably right. Pursuing O'Bannon would ignite a string of events that I would have to see through to the end. Open that door and there was no turning back. I drained my coffee and thought through my options. Time to find out who wanted me dead.

I FOLLOWED the directions to East Somerville. Vic's Automotive was near the intersection of Hawthorn and Arlington. The neighborhood was dense, houses packed on top of one another, with small businesses and restaurants thrown in for good measure.

I parked across the street from the shop's two-story high garage door. A freshly painted steel door, the main entrance to the shop, flanked the garage door on the right. I gripped my .45, keeping it inside my jacket, approached the front door and listened. The occasional screeching of a pneumatic something confirmed the place was open for business. I waited for the tool to fire up again before checking the knob. It was unlocked. Slowly opening the door, I peeked my head inside.

The inside of the shop was much cleaner than I thought it would be. I figured it would be littered with rusting auto parts and would reek like gasoline and grease, but it didn't. It seemed like a respectable operation, someplace you wouldn't be ashamed to take the family minivan for routine maintenance.

A dozen vehicles, all in various states of repair, lined the left wall. The remnants of an SUV's steel skeleton, which must have been picked clean for parts, sat along the right wall. On the left of the SUV was some sort of office, with a long glass window. To the right of the SUV was a Porsche Cayenne. A glimpse of the license plate confirmed it was the same vehicle that sat outside my house last night. I was in the right place.

The pneumatic wrench—I assumed it was a wrench— screamed again, and this time an air compressor the size of a refrigerator kicked on. I followed the red hose from the compressor across the floor and underneath a hydraulic scissor lift supporting a black Mercedes in the middle of the shop. I walked toward the Mercedes to get a better look, staying away from the office window to my right. A pair of legs moved underneath the sedan and the tool whirred again.

I gripped the .45 tight and leaned forward far enough to see two men sitting in the rear of the office watching a game show on a small television. Opening the office door, I raised the weapon and approached them from behind.

They both turned around at the same time, probably seeing my reflection in the television screen.

"Where can I find Alfie O'Bannon?" I asked, taking aim at the bigger of the two.

The other man spoke up first. "No clue. He never comes around here."

"Who's under the Mercedes?"

"That's Mouse."

"He know where O'Bannon is?"

"Maybe."

"The shop is closing early," I said. "You two are gonna disappear for an hour or so. Come back any earlier, and I'll kill you."

"Okay," they said, standing up.

I moved to the opposite side of the room, putting enough

space between us so they wouldn't be able to get to me before I got a shot off.

"Quietly," I whispered as they walked onto the shop floor.

The tool underneath screamed again. Once the two men were gone, I made my way to the other side of the scissor lift. A man, a large one by the size of his legs, was halfway under the vehicle, working away. I stood between his legs waiting for the tool to die down. As soon as it did, I tucked the .45 into my waistband, grabbed his pants legs just below the knee, and heaved him out from underneath the car.

"What the hell?"

The man in the navy blue coveralls with the confused look on his face was covered in tattoos, about six foot four, and as solid as me. At that size, I wondered how he got the name Mouse.

He'd be more dangerous on his feet, so when he planted his hands on the floor to push himself up, I stomped my boot into his ribs sending him back to the oil-stained concrete floor. I jerked my weapon out of my waistband and centered it at his chest to keep him on the ground.

I've thrust handguns into more faces then I can count, and I've seen a variety of reactions. Some cry or start speaking incoherently. Others drop to their knees and start praying like God gives a damn. Some faint. One attorney in Queens shit himself right there in the lobby of his law office. I'd seen all kinds of expressions, but the calm look on Mouse's face was a rarity. He wasn't rattled. He almost seemed comfortable staring down the barrel of the .45, as if it were nothing more than a tattoo gun.

"Who the fuck are you?" he said.

"That's not important. Where can I find Alfie O'Bannon?"

He wiped his dirty hands down the sides of his coveralls, leaving dark streaks on his thighs.

"You stepped in it deep, friend," he said, looking me in the eyes. "You know what's gonna happen to you for coming in here like this?"

"Where's O'Bannon?"

"I'm not telling you anything."

Mouse lurched for something underneath the car, maybe the wrench or some other tool, but I drove my two-inch boot heel into his stomach. He rolled onto his side clutching his gut. Then, mustering whatever resilience my size twelve hadn't driven out of him, he tried to get up. He was almost to his knees when I clocked his jaw with the butt of my .45. He went back down, his head bouncing off the concrete floor. His eyes fluttered shut, and a moment later he was out.

When he came to he groaned, tried to get up again, and then realized his new predicament. A man that size makes a lot of noise.

I pressed the button on the yellow controller in my hand and a high-pitched hum cut through his screams as the scissor lift, still supporting the pristine Mercedes, inched closer to his face.

"How much you think this car weighs, Mouse?"

He instinctively turned his head as the bottom of the lift approached the tip of his nose. I pressed the red button, bringing the yellow lift to a stop against his cheekbone.

He screamed again, but it was muffled this time on account of the hyperventilating.

"Get it off!" His legs kicked wildly, like an insect on its back.

"I'll raise it when you tell me where O'Bannon is."

"At his place on Dartmouth." He struggled to breathe. "Busted Knuckle."

"Thanks for the information, Mouse." I tossed the scissor lift control box through the Mercedes's open driver window.

"I'll be back in a minute."

"I told you where he is. Get this off of me."

I left Mouse underneath two tons of fine German craftsmanship, walked to the front garage door, and raised it. A minute later I was backing my Jeep into the center of the garage. A minute after that, I was hauling Lucky Walsh's now-stiff corpse out of the back of my Jeep and across the shop's concrete floor. The slick tarp made it easy to drag.

I slid it into the office and rolled it into the corner next to the television. I had wrapped it tight, and now it looked like a shiny, blue cocoon.

Mouse's legs were still kicking when I returned to the Mercedes. The scissor lift had him pinned tight, but he was sweating like a waterfall, and if he got slick enough, he might be able to wriggle free. I'd be long gone by then.

"Get it off!" he yelled.

"I can't have you gunning me down on my way out, so you'll have to wait. Scream loud enough and someone's bound to hear you."

I was halfway to my Jeep when I turned back.

"Oh, and Mouse? There's a dead body in your office. If O'Bannon's not where you said he is, I'm coming back here, and I'll stack you next to it."

I climbed into my SUV and rolled out onto Hawthorn Street. Time to go see Alfie O'Bannon.

6

FALSE ALARM AT THE BUSTED KNUCKLE

I WAS in the US Army's Military Intelligence Corps for twenty years. When I retired, I got a fancy plaque and a letter signed by the president. One of my core responsibilities in MI was gathering human intelligence, or HUMIT if you want to sound smart. A HUMIT information gathering session has five phases: planning and preparation, approach, questioning, termination, and reporting. I didn't have time for all that with Alfie O'Bannon. I planned to skip right to questioning. According to Mouse, O'Bannon was at the Busted Knuckle on Dartmouth. That's only a mile or so away.

Finding O'Bannon was one thing, but getting the information I wanted was going to be something entirely different. Mr. Fish said O'Bannon was an old mobster, and old mobsters are tough to crack. They just don't give a shit.

The Busted Knuckle was a greasy-spoon diner built in the Art Deco style. Two large windows flanked the front doors, which were outlined with thick metal trim. The door handles were shaped like saucers. I stepped inside and the smell of sausage hit me in the face. I hadn't been hungry when I walked in, but now I wasn't so sure.

Tables with green tops and silver edging lined the right wall, which was dotted with black and white photographs hung at irregular intervals. A counter about thirty feet long was on the left, with the kitchen behind it. This place hadn't changed since the 1930s and had an unintentional trendy vibe. It probably attracted more hipsters than mafiosos, but that was likely due to the gentrification of the neighborhood, not a formal business plan.

I took a stool at the end of the counter where it turned ninety degrees into left the wall. From my seat, I not only had a clear view of the back of the place, but I could still keep an eye on the front door. If Mouse got free from the scissor lift, he might take it upon himself to call his boss, or even barge through the doors of the Busted Knuckle looking to stop me from doing whatever it was he thought I was here to do. If that became a reality, I wanted to see him coming.

An older man wearing a stained white apron approached and asked if I wanted a menu.

"Just a coffee," I said.

A moment later, I was sipping the strongest coffee I'd ever had. I kept the chipped ceramic mug close to my face and looked the joint up and down. There were maybe thirty people having breakfast. It didn't take long to pick O'Bannon out of the crowd. He sat in the back of the restaurant, away from the other customers. It wasn't his seating choice that gave him away. It was the two bodyguards sitting next to him. Both outweighed me by at least fifty pounds. They looked like boxers who were past their prime. A bit out of shape, but still capable of delivering some serious damage if they had to.

I waved the man in the apron over and asked where I'd find the bathroom. He pointed his metal spatula toward the rear of the restaurant. Setting the mug back on the counter, I stood up and walked toward O'Bannon. I manufactured an impromptu limp as I moved down the bar. The limp allowed me to move slower than someone usually would, giving me ample time to survey the back of the place.

O'Bannon's private dining area looked like a place you'd rent out for large parties. His table was the only one back there, so no one would make the mistake of grabbing a nearby seat. Behind O'Bannon and his men was a door that led out the back. To the right of the door was a waist-high stand stacked with glassware. Next to that was a tall garbage can, and above that was a fire alarm.

The bodyguards clued in on me when I got within thirty feet of O'Bannon. I only got a glimpse of the old man. I could tell he was thin and frail, even though his black jacket was zipped halfway up his chest. His white hair was neatly combed, and he wore thick, black-rimmed glasses that made him look like a record producer. His protection detail didn't stand up, but their eyes cut through me, a warning that I was approaching no-man's-land. Had I kept coming, one of them would have intercepted me, but I wasn't going to get that close. Not yet.

They watched as I limped closer, but then I turned and hobbled into the men's room. I waited for a few minutes inside the bathroom and then stepped back out into the restaurant. A young man, maybe twenty years old, blew past me carrying two black garbage bags. He stepped past O'Bannon, who paid him no attention, and went out the back door. Just as I made it back to my stool, the young man was returning through the door empty-handed.

I choked down the rest of the coffee, dropped a five-dollar bill on the bar, and left. A block later, I dropped the limp and returned to my Jeep.

I GRABBED my .45 from underneath the driver's seat and screwed on the suppressor. I hoped I didn't have to use it, but a suppressed weapon creates a vivid psychological effect. It says, "I'm prepared to shoot you and I've thought ahead."

I slipped it inside my coat and tucked it under my left armpit. Then I locked up my Jeep and took an alley to the rear of the restaurant.

It wasn't going to take some sophisticated scheme to get to O'Bannon. His security was a joke. There were no cameras in the restaurant and he was sitting out in the open, directly in front of what I hoped was an unlocked door. His bodyguards looked intimidating, but that's what mob bodyguards do, look intimidating. When the guns come out, they're usually not much help.

Old-school mobsters like O'Bannon rely on their reputation to keep threats away. It's likely everyone in that restaurant, hell, maybe everyone in the neighborhood, knew who he was and what he does. No one in their right mind would touch him.

Except me.

I surveyed the back of the building. Modern businesses typically connect their fire alarms into wireless networks. The alarm goes off and the system either sends a signal to an alarm monitoring company that dispatches the fire department or it sends the signal directly to the firehouse. Either way, it's a wireless system and there isn't much you can do to stop that signal from going where it's supposed to go. The Busted Knuckle didn't have a wireless system. I saw the two fire alarm pull stations mounted to the wall inside, and neither had an antenna. They did have wires running up the wall though. That meant they were connected into the phone line. The result is the same, a direct line to someone paid to put out fires, except the signal goes through the phone line instead of a wireless network. And phone lines can be cut.

I followed the phone lines down the side of the Busted Knuckle's exterior wall where they fed into a junction box. I jerked on the beige wires and all six tore free from the junction box, the jagged bare ends each pointing in a different direction.

Taking a deep breath, I checked the back door. Had it been locked, my plan would be dead on arrival. Luckily, the busboy didn't lock the door when he came back in from his garbage run. I opened it slowly and slipped in. O'Bannon and his two bodyguards had their backs to me. Keeping my eyes on them, I felt my left hand across the wall until I found the pull station and yanked. A piercing alarm shot through the restaurant and two bright lights flashed above each pull station. It took a few seconds for the first customers to stand up and begin to evacuate through the front door, but as soon as the first few got up, the rest followed their lead. The kitchen staff even walked out with their aprons still tied around their waists.

O'Bannon's bodyguards stood up to help him out of his chair, but I closed the gap between the back door and the table.

"Sit down," I said, removing the .45 from underneath my coat.

O'Bannon saw the weapon and motioned his men to sit down. I grabbed the empty chair next to O'Bannon, slid it about five feet back from the table and took a seat, my .45 propped up on my right thigh. He probably knew I wasn't there to kill him. There's no chitter-chatter in a mob hit. They're fast and furious. Had I been there to murder him, I'd have walked in, emptied my magazine into all three of them, and disappeared out the back door within fifteen seconds. The fact I sat down had already set him at ease.

"This isn't how sit-downs are supposed to work, son," said O'Bannon, practically yelling to speak over the fire alarm. "What you want?"

"Information."

"Then go buy a newspaper."

I pulled my cell phone from my pocket with my free hand and slid it to the middle of the table. Lucky Walsh's lifeless grin stared up at him.

"He blutered or dead?"

The fire alarm siren stopped, but the two lights kept flashing. No large red trucks were going to respond thanks to the severed phone lines, but I figured I had five minutes or so before the patrons wandered back in realizing it was a false alarm.

"He's dead," I said.

"That's not good for you."

The bodyguard closest to me gripped the sides of his chair, his forearm muscles tensing. He was prepping to lunge at me. When he slid his legs further underneath his seat so he could spring out of his chair, I pulled the trigger. The slug went through his shin, shattering his tibia. The blow knocked him backward and he fell to the ground screaming. The other bodyguard stood up, but I raised the .45 toward his chest and he sat back down.

"Am I supposed to just let ya come into my place and start killing people?"

"I haven't killed anyone. Yet." I moved the weapon toward O'Bannon. "Tell me who put a contract out on me and I'll go away."

"I don't even know who you are, son."

"Connor Harding."

The old man adjusted his glasses, studied my face, and nodded. "I got nothing else to say to you," he said.

"Since you sent someone to kill me, I won't feel bad handicapping you, Alfie. You're going to tell me who called it in."

"Fuck off. You don't have the balls."

I fired again, this time blowing a hole through O'Bannon's calf. He fell out of his chair. The remaining bodyguard jumped up, reaching for a weapon he had tucked inside his jacket. My third shot tore through his shoulder, dropping him to the ground. His piece slid across the floor toward the bathroom.

"You made a terrible mistake," said O'Bannon, pressing a white linen napkin against his bleeding leg.

"Someone's already out to kill me, Alfie. Anything I do here isn't gonna make my situation any worse." I pressed the .45 into his side. "I'm going to ask you one more time. Who authorized the hit?"

He didn't say anything.

I pulled the hammer back. "Three seconds, Alfie."

Nothing.

"Two. One."

"Alright. Sontag's crew called it in."

"Joseph Sontag?"

"Yes!"

The first few patrons returned to the restaurant. I pulled the

.45 back, grabbed my cell phone off the table, and slipped out the rear door. Half the kitchen staff was probably armed, and I didn't want to be anywhere near the place when they found O'Bannon and his bodyguards. I ran down the back ally, climbed into my Jeep, fired the engine, and pulled into traffic.

Joseph Sontag was bad news. He ran one of the three New York City crime clans. And if he wanted you dead, you didn't have much time left. I should know. I used to work for him.

7

JOSEPH SONTAG

JOSEPH SONTAG WAS one of New York City's most feared mob bosses. He ran the Sontag Clan from the early nineties until his arrest three months ago. The FBI took him into custody outside his headquarters on the Upper East Side. According to the papers, they used twenty-two agents armed with flak jackets and assault rifles. Sontag was alone.

All the major networks ran segments on the aging mob boss, who had attained a kind of mythical status. The Boston Herald ran a four-page spread on his life in the NYC underworld. Don't get me wrong, the arrest should have been headline news, but not because of who Sontag was or what he'd done from atop NYC's criminal food chain. What was more appealing, to me anyway, was that the FBI was finally able to take down the head of one of the most ruthless crime clans in recent memory, a man whose reputation for evading capture was as notorious as his appetite for violence.

Sontag's longevity was due to his willingness to do anything to expand his territory and stay in power, as well as the unprecedented loyalty he had from his men. I'd seen looser lips in military intelligence than I had in Sontag's operation.

The old man structured his organization similar to other Mafia families, with one key difference. While other outfits used an underboss to manage the day-to-day activities of the family and serve as a buffer between the boss and the capos, Sontag preferred to run things himself.

Underneath Sontag were five individuals he called "managers." They were: Nicky Sontag, his son; Declan Porter; Victor Tan; Frank Astassi; and Collin Roth. Each of these managers ran a crew of twenty men, no more, no less, and reported directly to Sontag. The individuals under the managers were known as "employees." Managers could socialize with one another but were forbidden to discuss business with other managers, so no one knew what anyone else was doing. Sontag believed if managers and employees were only privy to their individual twenty-man operation and not the workings of the clan as a whole, there was less chance they could provide the authorities with enough detailed information to bring him down.

So, where did I fit in? I worked for Sontag for six years, but you wouldn't find me on any formal org chart. I didn't have a specific title, but Sontag referred to me as his Mirage Man. That's the sexy description, but mostly I was a freelance problem solver, a repairman. Someone who put the pieces back together when things fell apart.

Sontag kept me employed because my background in MI gave me a skill set he required, but only from time to time. So it wasn't unusual for me to disappear for weeks at a time. I didn't associate with many others in the organization when I was off the clock, but I was always on call.

I reported to Sontag personally, and while I kept my business separate from the other managers, I did work with them on occasion, usually to mop up after one of them, or one of their employees, fucked up.

Most of the managers didn't like having me around. They regarded me the same way most cops looked at the internal affairs division. A necessary evil, but someone they'd rather not encounter too often. They didn't like the idea I was a freelancer who was not as committed to the clan as everyone else. They also didn't like that I wasn't a "made" man. I never swore allegiance to the family, and I never looked at my role as a lifetime position. Sontag trusted me, and that's all that mattered, even if the other members of the organization didn't.

Trust and secrecy were priority one for Sontag. Over the years, he'd seen the feds surgically dismantle several criminal organizations for making stupid mistakes.

He'd been an up-and-comer in eighty-nine when the feds took down the heads of all the Italian families. Those storied organizations crumbled quickly after the purge, creating a void that opened the door for new bosses and clans that had no Italian affiliation. Eager criminals flooded the market, and over time they fought it out. The dominant, more violent and organized groups rose to the top, and then crushed their competition until there were only three clans left to control the five boroughs.

Sontag knew what the FBI was capable of, and while fear and intimidation kept his men in line, it did little to deter the FBI from looking into his activities. He knew the feds could monitor any electronic conversation, so Sontag never communicated by telephone, email, or text. Sontag conducted all of his discussions in person, meeting with his managers each morning at an ever-changing location to prohibit any rooftop or park bench surveillance. He'd talk about the business of the day, return to his headquarters, and then do it all over again with the next manager. New man, new location. Unless the FBI blanketed the entire island of Manhattan with field agents, there was no chance of getting a clear peek into Sontag's operation.

These precautions kept the FBI on the outside for decades. When they finally cuffed him that Tuesday morning three months ago, everyone assumed someone on the inside of his organization had cooperated with the feds. But who?

I left my position as Sontag's Mirage Man with the boss's blessing, retiring to Boston two years ago. But good terms can turn bad real quick, especially if when Sontag got popped he thought I had something to do with it. O'Bannon implicated Sontag's crew as putting out the contract on my life, but that didn't mean the old man called it in. If it wasn't Sontag, then it was one of his managers. My operating theory was that someone was tying up loose ends, eliminating anyone who might be able to testify against Sontag. It's a solid strategy.

Mob hits usually go smoothly. This one was an utter clusterfuck. That didn't mean it was over. Once it got back to the shot caller that things didn't go as planned, they'd regroup and come again, but it would be worse this time. Thanks to my necessary stunt at the Busted Knuckle, the next wave wouldn't be as civilized as two shots to my head. They'd try and take me alive, strap me to a chair in a musty basement, and start cutting things off. I wasn't going to let that happen, which is why I had to go the NYC and see Sontag.

My plan was to contact Sontag and find out if he called it in. If he did, and Sontag was the type of person who'd tell you to your face if he wanted you dead, then I'd have to talk him out of it, get him to call it off. Given everything I'd done for him over the years, I was confident I could convince him I wasn't a threat. I could make a deal with him.

The other possibility was someone in his organization was mopping things up, with or without Sontag's knowledge. If that was the case, Sontag still had the authority to cancel the hit.

Regardless who was behind it, I needed to get to NYC and talk to Sontag in person. And that meant seeing the one person who might be able to arrange such a meeting. Declan Porter.

Porter was one of Sontag's managers and one of the few people in the city I trusted. Talking to any of Sontag's managers could be dangerous, because it was likely one of them was responsible for shutting me up permanently. But it wasn't Porter. Before Declan Porter became one of Sontag's managers, he was his top enforcer, responsible for more deaths than I can count. If Porter was running point on taking me out, he wouldn't have farmed it out. He would have done it himself.

And he would have succeeded.

8

DECLAN PORTER

THE LAST TIME I saw Declan Porter, he was holding a gun to my head. He didn't pull the trigger then, and I hoped he wasn't looking to pull it now. Aside from Nicky Sontag, Porter was one of Joseph Sontag's longest-standing managers. He'd been a part of the organization for as long as I could remember, and if someone was out to shut me up, he'd likely know about it.

In addition to running a variety of rackets for Sontag, Porter also operated KORK, a wine bar on the corner of 83rd and 3rd on Manhattan's Upper East Side. He sold overpriced wine to investment bankers and other types who like to buy expensive things.

Porter was the kind of person other people wanted to be around, even if they were aware of what he did for a living. That was his appeal. Much like O'Bannon holding court at the Busted Knuckle, Porter drew crowds, and sometimes Sontag's ire, at KORK. Sontag had remarked to me on multiple occasions that he thought Porter was too flashy, too arrogant, and too committed to his side business. Porter got a pass though because KORK is how Sontag laundered most of the clan's money. As long as Porter kept the money clean and flowing, Sontag would let him get away with almost anything.

It took me four hours to drive to New York City; the lump formed in my throat somewhere near Hartford. I found a parking spot on Third Avenue and walked the three blocks to the bar. Porter always parked his car directly outside the front door next to a bright white reserved sign. Manhattan didn't allow reserved parking spaces on public streets, with this exception. Before I retired, Porter was driving a black Mercedes, much like the one I nearly used to crush Mouse's head. It looked like Porter drove a silver Jaguar now.

I was walking a delicate line by going to see him, and our conversation could go a few different ways. One, he'd tell me he didn't know anything about the contract. They teach you a variety of skills in MI, and spotting a liar is intelligence gathering 101, so I'd see through any bullshit he slings my way. Two, he's aware of the contract but can't, or won't, feed me any details. Three, he tells me who called in the hit and why. This was as likely as Lucky Walsh tap dancing on the Great Wall of China. Or, four, he'd shoot me on the spot and everything else was moot.

Porter was a loyal soldier and didn't owe me a damn thing, so on the one hand there wasn't much reason to believe he'd tell me anything. I had nothing to hold over his head for leverage, but we did have history, and sometimes history is all you need.

KORK hadn't changed much. A long, cherry bar lined the left wall. Along the right side were two dozen tables, each with a single votive candle and two plush black-and-white chairs. Large, gilded-framed oil paintings, like those you'd find in a museum, hung on the maroon walls. The stone busts were new since last I'd been here. Under the eight crystal chandeliers, the bar and tabletops shined like a cadet's shoes. Men in expensive suits and women in short dresses filled the place, talking about whatever beautiful rich people talked about.

I crossed the lobby, no one paying me any attention in my dark-green military jacket and jeans. At the hostess stand, a woman with shoulder-length blond hair cut in the straightest line I'd ever seen adjusted her tight, black sequined dress. I rapped a knuckle on the wooden stand and she whirled around so quickly on her thin stilettos she almost lost her balance.

"I'm sorry," she said. "I didn't see you there. Can I help you?"

"I'd like to see Declan Porter."

She took a step backward and searched her brain for whatever canned response they told her to say when someone like me asked to see Porter. After a moment, she found it.

"Mr. Porter isn't here right now."

"Isn't that his Jag outside?"

She fidgeted with the maroon, leather-bound menus in front of her.

"It's okay," I said. "We're old friends. He'll see me."

The woman turned and walked to the back of the bar, her hips swaying back and forth like a metronome. After a few minutes, a man in a gray suit approached from the left. I made him as soon as he stepped out of the side room that flanked the front door. He moved behind me, but I sidestepped and turned to keep him in front of me.

"Something I can do for you?" He didn't smile.

"The lovely lady is helping me," I said.

"And now I'm helping you."

"I'm here to see Porter."

"He's not—"

"Of course he's here. Tell him Connor Harding wants to speak with him."

"Who?"

"Connor Harding." I spoke slower this time.

"Who are you with?"

"At the moment, I'm with you. But I'd rather not be."

The man grinned, backed away, slipped a cell phone from his pocket and dialed.

After clicking off the phone, he signaled me to follow him and we started toward the back of the bar. He led me up a wrought iron, spiral staircase to the second floor, where another large man, this one wearing a black hoodie instead of a suit, patted me down. He slipped the 1911 Springfield Armory .45 out from my shoulder holster, ejected the magazine and the chambered round like it was routine, and set it on a table.

"You're not coming to kill me with that are you?" said Declan Porter, emerging from a door behind me.

"I hadn't planned on it."

"What are you doing back in New York? That's not how exile works." He smiled.

"I'm not in exile. I'm retired."

"The forty-five says otherwise." He looked me up and down. "What do you want?"

"Is there someplace more private we can talk?"

Porter led me down a hallway and the man in the suit followed. In his office, Porter sat behind a desk thick enough to catch a bullet. I eased into a padded leather chair. The man in the suit stood next to the door with his hands on his hips.

"You don't need the extra security," I said. "I'm just here to talk."

"Actually, I do. It's been a bit savage around here lately. With Sontag in the poke, shit's escalating."

"That's why I'm here. Someone tried to put me down the other day."

"How?"

"Sent a triggerman to my house."

"It's a cold trade we're in, my friend. But he obviously didn't succeed."

"I got lucky."

"And you're here because you think I had something to do with it?"

"Did you?"

"No," he said, looking sincere.

"You know Alfie O'Bannon?" I asked.

"Of course, I know him. He's the one who sent a man after you?"

"That's right. He said it came from you guys."

"He told you that?"

"Yeah. After I put a slug through his leg."

"You shot Alfie O'Bannon? Jesus Christ, Connor. Not good."

"He wouldn't talk otherwise. Said your crew called it in."

"Well, I didn't do it. I got no beef with you."

"What about Sontag? I thought we were square when I left. He have a change of heart?"

"No change of heart as far as I know. Your terms are still good."

I glanced back toward the office door. If Porter had wanted me dead, the muscle in the gray suit would have already blown my head off.

"O'Bannon wasn't acting on his own," I said, turning back to Porter.

"He told me you guys were behind it. Maybe Sontag put the contract out and didn't tell you."

"He didn't call it in. He'd tell me. You got another theory?"

"Maybe someone is acting on their own to protect him. They want to take me out and keep whatever information I have quiet."

"I'd know about it if that were the case." He folded his arms. "Truth is, Connor, you're just not important enough to kill."

"That doesn't change the fact Alfie O'Bannon sent someone after me, and he told me Sontag's crew ordered it."

Porter didn't say anything, and for the first time, I thought he knew something he wasn't telling me.

"What about Nicky?" I said.

Nicky Sontag was on my shortlist. He didn't like that I left New York with his father's blessing, was always vocal about me being a liability, and he'd have the authority to utilize the clan's assets to take me out.

"When all this happen?" asked Porter.

"Yesterday."

Porter shook his head. "Nicky's got his own problems. It wasn't him."

"What kind of problems?"

"That's privileged information. Employees only."

"Look, the way I see it, you've got a real problem here, and it'll be better if we work together."

"How is someone gunning for you *my* problem?"

"The issue is that someone is moving on me, and probably other associates too, and you don't know about it. And if you've still got Sontag's ear, then you *should* know about it. That means someone is tapping into the clan's assets and signing contracts without the proper authority."

I watched as Porter connected the dots in his head.

"You've got a rogue agent on the payroll, Porter."

He pointed to the man in the gray suit and ordered him out of the room.

"It's not Nicky," said Porter, his voice lower than before. "He's not concerned about you at the moment."

"How do you know?"

"He's not calling anything in. He's been in hiding for weeks."

"Why?"

"If Sontag goes to prison, Nicky takes over the family. Some people don't want to see that happen."

"Someone move on him?"

"Car bomb. It detonated early. Nicky wasn't even close to it. Took out a bodega and part of a library in Alphabet City. Nicky disappeared before they got a second chance."

"They've got to be connected, the hit on him and me."

"Maybe they are, maybe they aren't."

"You looking into it?"

"I'm focused on dismantling the feds' case and making sure Sontag never goes to trial. If I do my job, Sontag gets released, Nicky won't need the promotion, and this all goes away."

Porter didn't have to explain that with Sontag on the inside, a power struggle was brewing in the clan. Someone was looking to take over the operation, and Nicky, who was the rightful heir to the throne, had to go.

"With Sontag gone, I'm trying to keep this whole operation

from crumbling down, and I don't have the resources to figure out who's aiming to be the last man standing."

"You don't have that many names in the hat. If it's not you or Nicky, that leaves Victor, Frank, or Collin."

"Who says it's a manager? Could be any hothead in the organization. Shit, it could even be one of the other clans trying to dismantle us from the inside."

He folded his hands, rested them under his chin, and stared through me.

"Maybe we can help each other, Connor. I don't have any leads to give you, except for the news on Nicky. Do what you do, and see what you can find out. If you get anything solid, let me know and I can put a stop to it."

"You're giving me the authority to investigate the operation?"

"I'm saying I won't kill you for asking questions about your situation. I won't kill you. That doesn't mean someone else won't. I suspect you understand what you're walking into here."

"I need to start at the top. I want to talk to Sontag."

"You have newspapers in Boston, right? Did you forget about the part where Sontag's in jail awaiting trial?"

"You have to have some line of communication with him."

"It's sporadic at best. He's got some privileges at MCC, but I can't just dial him up at will."

"Then get me inside."

"The only way you're getting inside a federal detention facility is to drive to the FBI field office and surrender to Uncle Sam under the RICO statute. Maybe they'll put you in the cell next to Sontag and you can ask him anything you want. Otherwise, my reach stops at that barbed wire fence."

"Then I'll have to start knocking on other doors."

"Be careful, Connor. This ain't no Agatha Christie novel. Start rattling trees and you'll have to deal with whatever falls out. And remember, not everyone appreciated the way you left things around here. I always liked you, but you won't get a warm reception outside this office."

"Noted."

"And there's something else. The feds are still building their case against Sontag. If you're in town rattling bushes, you're going to get their attention."

"This just gets better and better."

"You're the Mirage Man. You'll figure it out."

"Any suggestions on where to start?"

"While I can't connect you with Sontag, maybe his attorney can. Lyle Messner. You'll find him in Union Square."

"Lyle Messner," I repeated. "I hate that guy."

Porter pounded his desk twice. The office door opened and gray suit returned. Two meaty hands grabbed my shoulders and lifted me out of the chair.

"So, we're through here?" I said.

"I'm sorry about what happened, Connor. Let me know how I can help."

I thanked Porter, and the big man ushered me down the hallway where he returned my .45, minus the magazine and the spare round. He dropped those into his suit pocket. Then he nudged me down the spiral staircase and through the crowded bar to the front door.

"I've heard of you," he said, opening the door.

"That right? What have you heard?"

"That you get things done. And that you're an asshole."

"True on both counts," I said. "But you forgot the part about my razor-sharp wit. Some say it's my best quality."

He dropped the magazine and extra round into my jacket pocket, slapped me on the back hard enough to blur my vision, and pushed me out the door.

"Try not to get shot," he said.

9

THE LAWYER

I LEFT KORK and returned to my car. Lyle Messner wouldn't be at his office until tomorrow morning, which meant I had time to kill. I drove through Central Park and headed to the Hotel Beacon on the Upper West Side. I parked the Jeep in the Beacon's underground parking garage and swapped out my license plates for my old set of New York plates I kept under the back seat. They weren't legal, but if anyone was looking for a Jeep from Massachusetts, they weren't going to find it here. I wasn't too concerned about anyone scoping out my vehicle, but someone did try to launch Nicky Sontag into the stratosphere by way of a car bomb, so I figured I'd err on the side of caution.

Whenever I needed a hotel in the city, I always stayed at the Beacon. It was in a quiet part of town, which was hard to find in Manhattan, and it was close to a subway station in case I had to make a quick escape and couldn't get to my car. The Beacon was also one of the few hotels that still used physical keys, not key cards. Today, anyone can pick up an RFID card reader and writer on the dark web for less than fifty bucks.

With the right tools, all you have to do is swipe a used key card from a hotel's trash, spoof a master key using the card writer, and you've got instant access to any hotel room. It's surprisingly simple, and I didn't want anyone poking around my room while I wasn't there.

I checked into the hotel under an alias and requested a room with a king bed on the third floor away from the elevator. Inside the room, I unpacked my belongings and slipped a door wedge underneath the door. The wedge looked like a miniature high-heeled shoe, but instead of a heel, it had a thumbscrew that tightened against the floor rendering the door nearly impossible to open from the outside.

After a long shower, I laid in bed and thought about my conversation with Porter. At first, I thought Lucky Walsh came to kill me to shut me up—a preemptive strike to silence me before the feds pumped me for evidence they could use against Sontag during his trial. After talking with Porter, I realized the situation was more complicated.

Some eager beaver in the Sontag camp, or possibly in one of the other New York City clans, was exploiting the power vacuum Sontag's arrest had created.

Either someone inside the clan wanted to claw their way to the top of Sontag's organization, or someone outside the family wanted to bring down the organization from within so they could move in and take over Sontag's territory.

I didn't think someone outside the organization sent Lucky Walsh after me, because I was too far removed to be a threat. It made sense they might want to start an internal coup by taking out Nicky Sontag, but it made no sense to look for me. I doubt the other clans even remembered who I was.

That left someone on the inside. Nicky was in hiding,

deciding self-preservation was more important than company business. And from the looks of Porter's increased security, he was concerned for his own safety. I didn't know enough about the remaining managers' leadership ambitions to begin to place odds on who was the shot caller. Porter was also right when he mentioned it could be anyone in the organization, not just one of the other managers. Right now, there were too many possibilities to begin to create a game plan. I hoped talking to Sontag would provide additional direction, but before I could get to him, I'd have to talk to Lyle Messner.

I woke up at eight thirty, grabbed a cup of coffee in the hotel lobby, and hopped a cab to Messner's law office on East 14th Street near Union Square.

Lyle Messner had been Sontag's attorney for decades. He was a prick, but commanded a certain level of respect for his ability to keep Sontag out of prison for so long, at least until recently.

I entered the building's lobby and took the elevator up to the seventh floor. Messner's lobby resembled an English hunting lodge. The walls were covered in dark walnut, and three of the four walls had brass stag heads mounted on them. In the center of the lobby, two dark-brown leather sofas faced one another with a glass table between them. The vacant eyes of a ten-foot tall stuffed brown bear watched over the lobby from the corner of the main room. To the right of the bear was the receptionist's desk, and next to that was a double door that led to Messner's office. Off to the side was a large conference room with a long, shiny conference table surrounded by thick leather chairs, the kind with high backs and brass rivets.

I approached the desk and a young woman in a white blouse and navy blue suit jacket asked if she could help me. According to the brass nameplate on her desk, her name was Tabitha.

"I'd like to see Messner."

"And do you have an appointment?" She looked me up and down.

"I think we both know I don't. Let him know Connor Harding is here."

"He's with a client right now."

"I thought his client was in jail."

She adjusted her glasses. "He has several clients."

"Good for him." I motioned to the bear. "Are there a lot of grizzly bears in the city?"

"It's a Kodiak, not a grizzly. Mr. Messner killed it while on a hunting trip in Alaska and had it stuffed and shipped here."

"I'm sure the bear appreciates the change of scenery," I said. "I'll wait over there on that expensive couch."

"Your name again?"

"Connor Harding."

She picked up the phone as I sank into the leather cushion.

Twenty minutes later, four men, all wearing navy blue suits and short haircuts, walked out of the double doors. They glared at me as they passed, looking concerned, as though I was lowering the sofa's value by sitting on it.

After they loaded into the elevator, Messner approached. He wore a tailored light gray suit, orange tie, and a white shirt that was so crisp you could cut a finger on the collar.

"I thought you were dead," he said.

"You mean like the bear over there? What makes you say that?"

"Because one day you're here and the next you're not. And no one seemed to want to talk about it, so I just assumed they sealed you in a barrel and dropped you in the East River."

"I'm retired."

"No one in Sontag's outfit retires."

"I guess I'm bucking tradition. All I had to do was promise not to come back."

"Yet here you are." Messner motioned me back toward his office but stopped me next to Tabitha's desk. He gestured to her and she sprang out of her comfy office chair, walked behind me and pushed me against the desk, kicking my legs apart.

"What's with the third degree?"

"Just a precaution," he said.

She took my cell phone and weapon from inside of my jacket. The way she handled the .45 told me she did more than answer phones and file paperwork. After tossing the items into her top desk drawer, she ran her hands down the sides of my torso and legs but didn't find anything else of interest.

"You'll get these back on your way out," she said.

"Thanks," I said, following Messner into his office.

"Why are you back now?" He sat down at his desk. "And why come to my office?"

"I need to see Sontag. Porter said he's in MCC and that you might be able to get me in."

"If he believes that, Porter's drinking more than his customers. I can't help you, Connor. Sorry you wasted your time."

"You don't understand. Someone took a shot at me, and I need to talk to Sontag to find out why."

"Wait. You deserted the mob and then someone took a shot

at you?" He shook his head. "What a crazy upside-down world we live in."

"Cut the bullshit. Can you get me in to see him or not?"

"You understand he's locked inside a big concrete box, right? They don't have an open-door policy."

"You're his lawyer. You have to meet with him."

"Twice a week. Schlepping my ass down to Park Row is just one of the many perks I enjoy as Joseph Sontag's attorney."

"Take me with you to your next meeting. Tell them I'm your paralegal or something."

"It doesn't work that way, Connor. You can't just walk into MCC. You've got to be cleared by the Bureau of Prisons. They fingerprint you and confirm your credentials with the New York Bar." He slapped his hands on the desk and then raised them like a blackjack dealer ending his shift. "*Are* you registered with the New York Bar?"

I didn't say anything.

"I assume that's a no then."

"That's a solid legal deduction, asshole. I can see why Sontag keeps you on retainer."

"Piss off."

"There has to be a way to get me inside that facility."

"Except for a shovel or parachute, there isn't." He stood up. "Look, since you've been gone for a while, let me clue you in on something. The feds are still building their case against Joseph, and that means they're watching his entire organization. So what do you think is going to happen once they realize you're back in town sticking your head where it doesn't belong?"

"Funny, Porter warned me of the same thing."

"I guess he's not as stupid as I thought then. If you're not going to listen to me, then listen to him. Don't get wrapped up in this. You're just going to create more problems for yourself, and me."

"I'm not worried about the feds."

"Then you're a moron. I'm working every angle I can think of to get Sontag out of this shit, and I don't need you fucking anything up."

"I'm just asking for a meeting."

"Ain't gonna happen."

"What about a phone call? Can you get him on the phone with me?"

"No. Those conversations are recorded. You talking to Sontag is a fantasy. Let it go and move along. Go scurry back to whatever shithole you crawled out of."

Messner had a bad case of the hard-ass. Maybe he thought Tabitha confiscating my .45 in the lobby gave him the opportunity to talk all the shit he wanted. He was wrong.

His shoulders tensed as soon as he realized his tough talk wasn't sending me packing. I waited a moment and then charged the desk. It was heavier than I thought, but I threw my weight into it, sliding it across the hardwood floor and pinning Messner's legs between the desk and the volumes of leather-bound legal tomes on the built-in bookcase behind him.

He screamed and I slammed my right fist into his solar plexus. I didn't want to break anything, but I wanted to hurt him. The punch contracted his diaphragm, knocking the wind out of him. He fell forward onto his desk gasping for air and clawing his fingernails into the cherry top. He rose up, his legs still pinned against the bookcase and drew in all the breath he could. It sounded like he was choking on something. I'd taken a few of those shots myself, and it's one of the most intense pains you can experience. One shot would ruin his afternoon; two hits might send him to the hospital.

Messner's thick office doors swung open. I turned to find Tabitha charging me with a sawed-off shotgun. The thing looked like a tree trunk in her hands. She braced it against her shoulder and trained it at my gut. Then she looked past me to see Messner finding his breath again.

"Get the fuck out, Connor," he whispered.

Tabitha stepped a few feet back, still gripping the smoke pole in her hands. I can read people pretty well, and everything about this woman told me she wouldn't hesitate to blow me in two, not even for a second.

I raised my hands and walked out of Messner's office feeling Tabitha's heavy stare behind me. My cell was on top of her desk, but I had to open the desk drawer to find my .45. I picked it up with my thumb and index finger and slowly slipped it back into my shoulder holster. She inched closer to me as I grabbed the cell and retreated to the elevator. I could still hear Messner gasping for air in his office. She didn't lower the shotgun until sometime after the elevator door closed.

I walked out of the building's lobby faster than when I walked in. When I reached 14th Street, I threw my arm up and a cab pulled to the curb. I climbed in.

"Where to, friend?" The cabbie had a thick Middle Eastern accent.

"Harlem. One forty-two and Lenox."

He popped the cab into gear and squealed away from the curb, cutting off a delivery truck in the process.

I thought I'd get further with Messner, but given the security around MCC, I wasn't surprised he shut me down. While Messner was the first string I could pull to get next to Sontag, he wasn't the only one. I had another option.

A much more deadly one.

10

ZOE ARMSTRONG

JUST LIKE MR. Fish in Boston, I made a habit of knowing people who knew people. It was my version of professional networking, without the business cards or lunch and learns. Work in this business long enough and eventually you're going to need help, and it's better to know who to call before you need it.

Zoe Armstrong was the first person in my mental Rolodex. She was intelligent, savvy, and damn dangerous. A lethal combination. She was the type of woman who would charm your pants off and then shoot you in the kneecaps. She ran the Whisper Network, an underground information syndicate that provided intelligence and related services to all of New York City's criminal organizations. She was unique in that most everyone in the game was loyal to one organization or another. The large crime clans liked it that way because there was little chance of spilling trade secrets to the competition. Crossing family lines was often a death sentence, but not for Zoe. She played every angle, refusing to take sides and working for anyone who had the means to pay for her services. And the clans let her get away with it because she was too valuable to put out of business. They needed access to her list of services, even if monogamy wasn't on that list.

The brilliance of Zoe's operation was that no one knew who worked for her. She was plugged into every vein and artery in the city. Politicians, police, prostitutes, dealers, junkies, doormen, and paperboys. She knew how to work them all, which is why when it came to getting something she usually made it happen.

One of my last assignments before I retired was to recover four hundred grand from the trunk of a Lincoln sitting at the bottom of the Narrows. One of Sontag's bagmen was crossing the Verrazano Bridge en route to the clan's Brooklyn HQ when someone drove up alongside him and opened fire. I suppose the shooter was looking to relieve Sontag's man of his six-figure payload, but while blowing a driver to bits is an effective way to get him to stop his vehicle, doing it on a bridge isn't.

Instead of bleeding out and slowly coming to a stop on the side of the road, Sontag's man ripped through the bridge's barricade and plummeted into the Narrows. Four hundred grand isn't a write-off, which is why Sontag came to me. Then I went to Zoe. The next day, I handed my boss three hundred grand in wet bills. Zoe and I pocketed fifty grand each for our trouble. Finding someone who could locate the car in forty-five feet of dark abyss, crack the trunk, and retrieve the cash was one thing, but finding someone who could beat the NYPD scuba team to the bottom and then keep their mouth shout afterward was something else. I wasn't surprised she made it happen. That's what Zoe Armstrong did.

Zoe wasn't hard to find. She operated out of her jazz club,

Hoster Hall, in Harlem. It wasn't the Cotton Club, but it was dark, cozy, and the music wasn't bad either. The live jazz wouldn't start until eight o'clock tonight, but the doors were already open when I arrived around noon.

When I opened the door, the three men sitting at the bar winced and shielded their eyes as the sunlight burst in like a broken dam. I pulled the door closed and took a seat at the bar.

A lean, tall bartender in a black vest, white collared shirt, and black slacks tossed his *Sports Illustrated* magazine onto the bar next to me.

"What can I get for you?"

According to my watch, it was too early for scotch.

"Root beer," I said.

The bartender cocked his ear toward me as if he didn't hear me correctly. "Root beer? Like A&W?"

"Or Barq's. I'm not picky."

He waited for a moment to see if I was joking. Then he filled a rocks glass with ice, topped it off with the pistol-shaped soda gun, and set it in front of me. He rapped his fingers on the bar. "Want to open a tab, or are you one and done?"

I tossed a hundred on the bar and told him to keep it.

"Is Zoe in?"

The bartender stashed the bill in his vest pocket, crossed his arms, and propped his leg up on the three-compartment sink. "No. Might be back later though."

"I'll wait."

He nodded. "Take table twenty-two. Maybe she'll see you when she comes back."

I grabbed the glass and swiped an abandoned newspaper on my way to the back of the club. On the side of each table was a numbered bronze plaque the size of a checkerboard square. I struggled to read the table numbers in the dark, but I finally found table twenty-two at the back, next to the stage. The club was empty except for me, the bartender, and the three men at the bar. Not surprising. The club didn't serve food, and there was little reason to be at a jazz club with no jazz.

I leaned back in the hard chair and exchanged glances between the newspaper and the front door. An hour of reading and two root beer refills later, the barrel of a handgun pressed against the back of my head.

"Connor Harding. I almost forgot what you looked like from behind."

I turned around slowly to see my reflection in Zoe's mirrored sunglasses. She jostled a microphone in her hand.

"You almost gave me a heart attack," I said.

"I have that effect on people."

"How'd you know it was me?"

She nodded to a small smoke detector mounted to the ceiling—a video camera.

"You been here this entire time?" I said.

"No, I just got here."

"I've been watching the front door, waiting for you."

"Only assholes use the front door." She smiled. "How's Boston?"

"You keeping tabs on me?"

"Just like to know where all the game pieces are, that's all."

"I'm not in the game anymore."

She tapped the microphone on the left side of my jacket near my ribs. "Your forty-five says otherwise. I assume it's still a forty-five."

"Old habits."

"So why are you here? Our root beer isn't that good."

"There someplace private we can talk?"

Zoe led me around the back of the stage to a trapdoor in the floor. She swung it open, revealing a spiral staircase to the basement.

"After you," I said.

"No." She waited until I stepped down in front of her.

The basement was much brighter than the dim club above. Zoe had furnished the space like an apartment. There was a living room with a sofa, two chairs, and four video monitors, each linked to cameras in the club upstairs. Off to one side was a kitchen, next to that a bathroom, and then a door that led to a bedroom.

"You live here?"

"Sometimes." She dropped the microphone, grabbed a small gadget from her purse, and waved it around me.

"I'm not wearing a wire."

"Everyone who ever wore a wire said they weren't wearing a wire."

Satisfied I was clean, she dropped the device back into her purse. Even though Zoe was concerned about a listening device hidden somewhere on me, she dismissed the .45 she knew I had. She was either confident I wasn't here to kill her or had taken other precautions to ensure I wouldn't be successful if I were.

"Lot of people on edge around here," she said. "Don't know who you can trust anymore." She whipped her long black hair over her shoulder, sat on the sofa, and adjusted her sunglasses.

Zoe always wore sunglasses. She didn't like people seeing her eyes, though she never told me why. This pair, aviators with gold frames, was too big for her narrow face.

"So what can I do for you, Connor Harding?"

"I need to talk to Joseph Sontag."

"You know he's in federal holding, right?"

"I know. That's why I'm here. You have any connection there? Someone who can get me in?"

She fiddled with the leather strap on her purse. "Why do you want to see him?"

I told her about Lucky Walsh.

"You believe Sontag was behind it?"

I thought about Alfie O'Bannon writhing on the floor of the Busted Knuckle with a bullet hole in his leg. "I've got a solid lead that someone in Sontag's crew called in the hit, but I talked to Porter last night and he said he didn't know anything about it."

"You talked to Porter? He tell you about Nicky?"

"Yeah, which is why I'm thinking maybe the contracts on me and Nicky are connected."

"If I didn't know better, I'd say someone was thinning Sontag's herd," she said.

"Could be, but is it coming from inside or outside the family?"

"Hard to say. Maybe it's connected to the informant."

"What informant?"

"You talked to Porter and he didn't mention it?"

Zoe was normally tight-lipped. She'd either made a rare misstep or wanted me to think she had.

"He never mentioned anything about an informant," I said.

She hesitated for a moment. "Word is someone on the inside brought Sontag down. Porter is trying to suss out who."

"He said he was focused on disrupting the investigation against Sontag but didn't say anything about a mole."

"What better way to disrupt a federal investigation than eliminate the key witness?"

"Is that why Nicky went underground?"

"No one will ever convince me that Nicky flipped on his own father. No way. I don't know who it is. And I assume Sontag and Porter don't know either, otherwise NYPD would be finding body parts in all five boroughs." She ran her black fingernails up and down her jeans leg. "Maybe Sontag suspected it was you. Whoever it was gave the feds enough information to take him to trial. You'd have a lot of knowledge about the inner workings of the clan. Maybe Joseph thought you were the informant and sent this Lucky..."

"Walsh. Lucky Walsh. You think I'd talk to the feds?"

"No, but it really doesn't matter what I think, does it? The real question is whether Joseph believes you talked."

"All the more reason to chat with him face-to-face," I said. "So, can you get me inside or not?"

"Just to make sure we're on the same page here, you're asking me if I can get you inside a federal detention facility to meet with one of the most wanted men in New York?"

"That's about right."

"To be honest, I don't know about this one. Give me some time and I'll see what I can do. It's not a typical job."

"You don't deal in typical jobs, Zoe."

"I'll look into it. I might have a contact who can help, but no promises."

"No promises."

"What's a good way to reach you?" she asked.

I gave her my cell phone number. Zoe didn't write it down. She never wrote anything down.

"You can also find me at Hotel Beacon."

"Now why would I ever go to your hotel?"

"It's not a solicitation," I said. "But if we need to talk in person, you know where to find me."

"I'll keep that in mind. Go back to your hotel and wait for a call. If my guy can help, you'll probably have to do him a favor."

"Understood. Maybe you can help me with something else. Porter's convinced someone's making a power play for Sontag's throne. He asked me to look into it."

"Is that why you're really pumping me for information? You're working for Porter now?"

"I'm not working for anyone. I'm only concerned about who tried to off me, but if these two storylines are connected, investigating one might give me something on the other."

She nodded. "If you're asking me who tried to kill Nicky, I have no idea, but it's not surprising. Everyone knows he's weak."

"Everyone is weak compared to Sontag."

"Yeah, but Nicky isn't leadership material. If it wasn't for his old man, he'd have been run out of the city years ago. I wouldn't want to work for him."

"So you *do* think there's a power struggle?"

"Yes, I do. And my sources are telling me it's only a matter of time before Spiro and Napoli start scarfing up Joseph's territory."

Alfred Spiro and Armand Napoli ran the other two crime clans in New York City, and they were chomping at the bit to ravage Sontag's operation and claim it for themselves.

"That's bad news," Zoe continued. "If Joseph's clan crumbles and Spiro and Napoli control the city, then it'll be an all-out war until only one remains. Three clans keep the peace, but two is a clusterfuck waiting to happen."

"You backing a horse in this race?"

"I like Joseph. He's always been good to me, but who knows what the hell is going to happen with the Sontag Clan."

"You didn't answer my question."

Zoe adjusted her sunglasses again.

"No, Connor, I don't have a horse in this race. I'll keep on doing what I do regardless of who's running this city. That's the benefit of my situation. Nimble as a goddamn cat. I'll survive no matter who's in the driver's seat."

"You sure know a lot about what's happening around here."

"It's my business to know what's going on, and speaking of business, I've got some I need to get to. See yourself out, and keep that phone handy. My man will be in touch if MCC is a go."

I stood up and thanked her.

"And, Connor. Be careful. There's a lot of heat out there. I'd keep an eye over your shoulder."

"Why does everyone keep telling me that?"

"Because a lot has changed since you disappeared. There's landmines all over the place, and you're walking around in a pair of those big-ass clown shoes."

"I'll be as careful as I can."

"See that you do."

THERE WERE no cabs outside Zoe's club, so I started walking, keeping an eye out for darting yellow blurs. Before I could spot one, someone else spotted me.

The sedan pulled up behind me. Hugging the curb, its tires

rubbed against the street's gutter. I heard and felt it before I saw it.

"What are you doing around here?"

I turned around, slipping my hand inside my jacket. I didn't feel as though I was in danger—this was too public a place to take a shot at me—but the passenger's question did up my heartbeat.

"Just seeing an old friend," I said, stopping. "There a problem with that?"

"No problem, Connor."

The sedan was a Toyota Camry. The passenger was male, about mid-forties, and he hung out the window like he was reaching for something. The driver was also male, same age.

These guys wore suits. Most criminals don't wear suits or drive Camrys, which is why I relaxed a bit and left my .45 where it was.

"There something I can do for you?" I asked. "Or are you just keen to bother me?"

"What's your business with Lyle Messner?"

"Never heard of him," I said.

"You've never heard of Lyle Messner? Joseph Sontag's attorney?"

"Nope."

"Then why were you at his office an hour ago?"

"Don't know what you're talking about. You've got me confused with someone else. I suggest you put that car in drive and roll away."

"Nah. We don't have you confused with anyone, Connor Harding. We know who you are. Why are you back in New York?"

"I don't know what you're talking about." I started walking. The car pulled away from the curb and followed.

"You know, poking your head where it don't belong could get you in trouble, Connor. Especially if you're talking to Joseph Sontag's associates."

"I don't know what you're talking about, but if you want to park that car and step out, follow me down this alley here and we could discuss it further."

"Maybe another time, Connor. We got places to be, but we'll be seeing you again soon, I'm sure."

"Bye," I said, waving over my shoulder.

"One more question. How's Albert?"

I stopped and went for my weapon, but the car sped off. The Camry had New York tags, but I didn't get the digits.

11

THE WHISPER NETWORK

THE CAMRY MADE ME UNEASY. I didn't recognize the passenger or driver, and they weren't ready to tell me who they were, but they did intend to rattle me. Albert is my father, and while he was nowhere near New York, they obviously knew who he was. I received the subtle threat loud and clear.

A cab picked me up a few blocks from Zoe's club and took me to the 79th Street subway entrance. Apparently, someone was watching me, and while the Camry sped off before I could make the plate, another vehicle might have picked up my tail. If someone was following me, I wasn't about to lead them to my hotel. I ducked into the subway entrance and took the Red Line to the next stop at 72nd Street and then walked the three blocks to the Hotel Beacon. It wasn't CIA-level counterespionage, but being underground for even a few blocks would throw off anyone tailing me on the street.

Back in my hotel room, I spent the rest of the afternoon figuring out my next move. I didn't know if or when I'd ever hear from Zoe's contact, and if I couldn't get in to see Sontag in person, I'd have to start looking elsewhere. The next logical step was to question Sontag's other managers. I'd ruled out Porter and Nicky, but any of the other three could have been on the other end of that phone call to Alfie O'Bannon.

I knew two of them fairly well. Victor Tan was a hothead. He was ambitious but damn loyal. Years ago, Sontag had a run-in with a *New York Post* reporter. The reporter wrote an article with the headline THE MODERN MOB. They even ran a photo of Sontag standing in front of his Brooklyn HQ. Kelly something-or-other snapped it. His name was right there under the photograph in small cursive letters. Sontag didn't like the idea of being in the paper. He didn't want the spotlight or the attention it brought to his operation. He wanted to send a message, but the reporter was off-limits.

Just like law enforcement, reporters are too high profile. You can go after them, sure, but then you're starting a war. The *Post* would have thrown every resource they had at Sontag, researching him up and down, writing about everything he did, and eventually, they'd break a story and the NYPD would take notice. It could be the beginning of the end, and Sontag was smart enough to know it. But the photographer, Kelly something, he was just a stringer and not tied directly to the paper. He was far enough removed that anything that happened to him, given enough time, wouldn't draw as much suspicion as going after the man with the byline.

The story goes that Sontag had Victor follow the photographer. It turned out he rode his bike through the city all day, like a bike messenger, except he didn't deliver packages, he took pictures. Six weeks later, after the heat had cooled, on Sontag's orders, Victor parked his SUV at the intersection of East 95th Street and 2nd Avenue one Wednesday morning. He waited for the photographer to leave his apartment in Spanish Harlem like he did every morning. Just as he peddled across the intersection, Victor slammed the accelerator and crushed him and the bicycle under his front axle. He was picking bits of that photographer's body out of his grill for two weeks.

I was never positive if the newspaper ever made the connection, but shortly after their photographer called in dead, whenever they slipped Sontag's photo into the paper, they never identified the photographer, just labeled it "staff photo."

Victor was high on my suspect list, but he was rarely alone and I'd have to find the right time to talk to him. A wrong move with Victor and this would be a short investigation.

Frank Astassi was next on my list. He was a holdover from the old days of NYC organized crime. He'd been a foot soldier for one of the Italian families, and when the FBI sent them packing, Astassi slipped through everyone's fingers. At that time, he wasn't important enough to draw the FBI's attention, and the Italians must not have cared to bring him with them when they aborted the city to lick their wounds and reorganize in Italy.

While he didn't ascend through the ranks with the Italians, Astassi made a name for himself in Sontag's organization. He knew how to run things and was a strong numbers man. He was the closest thing Sontag had to an accountant, and I know he personally persuaded Sontag to make certain high-risk financial moves that could have gotten him killed if they didn't payoff. But they always paid off. If he had told Sontag to buy $10 million worth of water balloons in the middle of winter, Sontag would have done it. And he would have turned a profit too.

The problem with Astassi was that he wasn't ambitious. He was almost as old as Sontag and was in the sunset of his career.

I couldn't imagine him making a run for a leadership position; he seemed content where he was.

That left Collin Roth. He was more of a mystery because he joined Sontag's organization only months before I retired. I'd only been in the same room as him twice, and while I was confident I could identify him in a lineup, I didn't know much about him. He was a gigantic red question mark.

I had a lot to noodle, but it would have to wait. I'd been running on pure adrenaline since Saturday night, and my tank was empty. I closed my eyes and drifted off to sleep about an hour after room service delivered my Cajun chicken sandwich for dinner.

My cell phone woke me at seven in the morning. It was Zoe.

"Be out front of your hotel at nine. Look for a red minivan. My man'll get you into MCC, but you're going to have to do exactly what he says. No questions asked."

"Okay."

"Nine o'clock sharp."

"I'll be ready."

"Good. Try to look like an attorney."

I stared at the ceiling for the next thirty minutes, collecting by thoughts. I climbed out of bed at seven thirty, ninety minutes until I had to be in the lobby. I grabbed a shower, got dressed, and went to the tenth floor for breakfast. I didn't eat much. My nerves were phoning it in, and the two cups of coffee I had at breakfast didn't help. The waitress brought the check at eight forty. I was in the lobby five minutes later.

I've been in this business for a long time, and aside from having a reliable sidearm, one secret to staying alive is showing up early. Fifteen minutes was just the right time to settle in and check your surroundings. Any earlier than that and you look suspicious, but fifteen minutes, that was Goldilocks.

The lobby was alive, just like the city beyond the glass front doors. Guests crisscrossed the white marble floor, some in a hurry and others not. A man in a black suit and yellow tie behind the front desk checked guests in and out.

Zoe said to "look like an attorney," and that was a problem. I only packed jeans, a few button-down flannel shirts, and two sweaters, nothing that was going to let me pass for a lawyer. Had she called me last night, I would have had time to pick up something in Midtown. Now, I only had time to shop in the lobby of the Hotel Beacon. Nothing else was open yet.

I couldn't be picky, only patient. After a few minutes, the solution walked through the hotel's front door. A well-dressed man about my size wearing sunglasses with wooden frames walked into the lobby and approached the line for the front desk. He looked annoyed, like he wasn't the type of person who usually waited in lines. The doorman opened the front doors for a bellhop, who pushed a four-wheeled luggage cart into the lobby. The cart carried two suitcases, four suits, and four neatly pressed white shirts. The bellhop parked the luggage cart along the wall adjacent to the check-in line, but out of the way of the foot traffic. He motioned to the man in the wooden frames that he'd be right back and walked to the concierge station, where he chatted up a striking redhead.

That was my chance.

I casually walked to the luggage cart and snatched a charcoal gray suit and white dress shirt off the thick brass bar. The guests in the lobby were too focused on their mobile phones or deep enough in conversation with each other to notice me. A moment later, I was in the lobby restroom wearing my new suit and dress shirt and stuffing my original clothes inside the Koala Kare diaper changing station in the handicapped stall.

It wasn't a perfect fit, but I looked more like an attorney than I did five minutes ago. Now, it was only my brown leather boots that could give me away. They'd have to do because wooden frames must have packed his dress shoes in his suitcase.

When I left the restroom, my suit's previous owner was handing his credit card to the man behind the check-in counter. Looking as natural as I could in another man's clothes, I walked through the front door onto Broadway and waited to see if the Whisper Network was as dependable as I remembered.

I didn't have to wait long. The red minivan pulled in front of the hotel at nine sharp. I motioned to the driver. The side door slid open and a thin man with three-day-old scruff stuck his head out of the vehicle.

"Name?"

"Connor."

"Get in."

He slammed the door shut behind me.

THE INSIDE of the minivan looked like a place where electronics went to die. Laptops, mobile phones, tablets, cables, and other digital gear littered the floor. There were two monitors mounted to the side of the vehicle above a makeshift desk supporting a keyboard and a dozen memory sticks. The vehicle's rear windows were blacked out, and someone had ripped out the back seats. It looked like a cross between a budget-strapped surveillance van and a pawn shop on wheels. A thin man with dark circles under his eyes sat on a folding chair. I sat on the floor.

We pulled away from the hotel.

The thin man looked me up and down. "I'm Cricket," he said. He pointed his thumb at the driver. "And this is Bob. So you want to get into MCC, huh?"

"That's right. Zoe says you can make that happen."

"I can make that happen, but not with those shoes." He pounded his fist on the back of the driver's seat. "Bob, hit the Cole Haan store. World Trade Center."

Bob took the next right.

Cricket leaned over and searched through a pale-blue plastic bin on the floor next to him. He pulled out an orange tie and tossed it into my lap. "Put this on."

I obliged.

"Sit up straight," he said, grabbing a DSLR camera. He took my photo, ejected the memory card from the camera and inserted it into the laptop at his feet. He moved fast, like he'd done this a thousand times.

Cricket snapped his fingers. "Tie, please."

I removed it and handed it back.

Something whirred nearby. Cricket brushed aside a pile of cables on the floor and picked up a printer small enough to fit in the palm of his hand. It was slowly spitting something out. As he waited for the printer, he spun around in his seat, placed his laptop back on his knees and typed away.

"What are you doing?" I asked.

"Registering you with the New York Bar Association.

Unless you're already a member. That would save us a lot of trouble."

I remembered Messner asking me the same thing. "No. Afraid not."

"Didn't think so." Cricket went back to work. His hands moved across the keyboard like a pianist on speed.

"Cole Haan," said Bob as the minivan stopped.

"Get yourself a pair of black shoes, socks, and a belt," said Cricket, opening the door. "Move quick. You've got seven minutes."

"Is this really necessary?"

"Details matter, Connor. And in this case, they could mean the difference between visiting MCC and getting booked there."

"Fine."

I ran into the store, found the first pair of black dress shoes I could, grabbed a pair of socks and a size thirty-six belt and returned to the minivan to find Cricket fidgeting with a plastic ID card. He examined the card and then dipped it into a cup of water.

"What's with the water?" I said.

"Gotta cool it."

He dried the ID card off on his pants and then ran it up and down a leather shaving strop to wear the edges.

"Here you go, Roger Mathers," said Cricket. "But your law firm buddies call you Rodge, because you're a douche."

I slipped it in front of my wallet.

"No, put it behind your credit cards," he said. "No one carries their bar association ID in the front of their wallet."

I placed it behind my auto insurance card and returned the wallet to my back pocket. As I slipped on my new black socks and wingtips, Cricket fumbled with something near his feet. He opened a trapdoor in the minivan's floorboard, lifted out a briefcase, and set it on his lap. He opened it and slipped a few file folders inside.

"Two minutes," said Bob, not turning around.

"Listen carefully, Roger Mathers. We'll drop you off across the street from MCC. You'll take this briefcase and walk through the front door. Approach the window and tell them you're there to see Sontag. Give them your ID. They'll check an approved attorney list, which you won't be on. When they ask why you're not on it, you tell them you just joined Sontag's legal team and the paperwork is probably in process. They usually have a schedule of all the visiting attorneys, but you won't be on that either. That's not a big deal because attorneys drop in all the time to see clients, and sometimes they don't call ahead. Look like you're supposed to be there and you'll be just fine. Once they buzz you through the first door, you'll go through a metal detector. They'll also inspect your briefcase. Now, here's the important part. Don't let anyone but Gerry touch this briefcase. He started his shift at nine, so he should be the only one there.

"Why does it have to be Gerry?"

"Because anyone else is going to arrest you for smuggling heroin into a federal facility. Gerry's our man. Give it to him, and you're gravy."

I guess this is what Zoe meant when she said getting into MCC would be risky and to do exactly what Cricket said. I wasn't a drug smuggler, and of all the work I did for Sontag, I never touched the stuff, but at the moment, this was the only way to get inside.

The minivan slowed and Bob pulled over to the curb.

Cricket tossed a comb in my lap and crossed his arms. I took the hint and styled my hair as best I could without a mirror. I handed the comb back to Cricket, who wore a smirk like a dissatisfied mother on her son's school picture day.

"It'll do." He slid open the side door. I started to get out and Cricket blocked me with his leg.

"Forgetting something?" He glanced down at my white Cole Haan bag.

The belt. I grabbed it and threaded it through my belt loops as quickly as I could, certain I'd missed at least one.

"What's your name, Connor?"

"Roger Mathers."

Cricket smiled. "Gravy." He paused. "Remember, only Gerry inspects the case."

"Right."

He dropped his leg and I climbed out.

"Nice suit by the way," said Cricket, stroking his chin. "Might be a bit short though."

"I didn't have a lot of options."

"Good luck. Hope you get what you need." Cricket slammed the door closed and the red minivan pulled away.

Bob had dropped me off two blocks from MCC. My hands were sweating so much I thought the case would slip out of my grip. I walked to the end of the street and crossed Park Row. I took a deep breath, wiped my hands down my slacks, pushed open the door and stepped inside the Metropolitan Correctional Center.

12

PRISONER #1053

THE METROPOLITAN CORRECTIONAL Center housed inmates awaiting trial, and a few who were serving brief sentences. The building stood seven stories high. The lobby was about the size of a dentist office waiting room. Small and compact. Easy to monitor. And monitor they did; stationary cameras mounted to the wall covered the lobby from every conceivable angle.

There were two sets of windows and interior doors in the lobby. One was for attorneys, law enforcement, and MCC staff. The other set was for everyone else. I stepped to the appropriate window and smiled at the woman behind the three-inch bulletproof glass. Time to find out if Roger Mathers passes muster.

Look like you belong. "Roger Mathers. Messner and Associates. Here to see Joseph Sontag."

She retrieved a folder from a nearby file rack, opened it, and scanned something inside.

"Mathers?"

"That's right."

The woman pulled her keyboard toward her and slapped

the keys while glancing up at a monitor. "M-A-T-H-E-R-S," she said as she typed. She adjusted her glasses and squinted at the screen.

This is taking longer than expected.

"You're not on the list," she said.

"Which list?"

"Any of them." She typed again. "I got nothing. You're not even on the approved counsel list."

"I just joined Sontag's legal team two days ago. Been locked in a conference room up to my eyeballs in case files." I remembered the shotgun-wielding receptionist from Messner's office. "Tabitha should have set it up."

The woman didn't say anything.

I waited her out.

"Is Mr. Messner with you?" she said.

"He'll be here later. He's at a deposition this morning. Told me to get started without him."

She stared at me through the glass. All I could do was smile back.

She'd let me in. I might not be on the official list, but the story is solid. Attorneys join and exit cases all the time. Criminals like Sontag have the right to speak to their attorneys, and the feds aren't going to risk a mistrial because they didn't let an attorney in to see his or her client. Any attorney worth their law books would jump on that. The woman behind the glass knew that too, which is why she'd let me in eventually. She was asking the right questions, and I was tossing back the correct answers.

A metal drawer I hadn't noticed before slid out of the wall in front of me. I set my briefcase on the ground, removed the clipboard and pen from the drawer and wrote down Mathers's name, Messner's law firm, the time I arrived, and who I was there to see. Then I opened my wallet and fished out my Cricket-issued credentials. I tossed it on top of the clipboard like it was something I'd done a thousand times before. I dropped the smile and replaced it with an annoyed expression. Something that said *I know this is routine, but I'm too important to wait this long.* That's how "Rodge" would feel.

The woman pulled the drawer back into the wall and reviewed the information. A loud buzz and a click followed. The door unlocked and I picked up the briefcase and walked from the lobby into a small hallway with a metal detector, a table, a blue garbage can, and another guard in a light blue shirt. Unless he pinned the wrong Federal Bureau of Prisons ID to his shirt, his name wasn't Gerry.

The woman behind the glass returned my ID through a small slit in another window. I slipped it back into my wallet and looked up to see Not-Gerry waving me toward the metal detector. The door to the lobby I'd just walked through clicked, locking behind me.

"Sir," said the guard, motioning me forward.

Did Cricket give me the wrong guard's name? Was Gerry his inside man at another facility? No way. From what I'd seen in that minivan, Cricket was a pro.

I walked through the metal detector with my briefcase. No beep.

"Sir, step over this way and place your briefcase on the table, please."

I did as he asked.

The guard slid the briefcase closer, popped open the brass locks, and opened it. He tilted it to the side and slowly jiggled it so all the items—including folders, pens, a notepad, an audio recorder and a takeout bag from a local Mexican restaurant—slid gently onto the table in front of him.

Shit.

I looked for some sign from Not-Gerry that everything was okay. A wink or a signal that expressed, *don't worry, this is just for show. We're all good.* That never came.

The guard ducked his head closer to the case as he felt around the inside seams where the bottom met the sides. Satisfied the case was solid, he began examining each item as if it was the first time he'd ever seen them. He thumbed through the legal pad and placed it back into the case. Then he picked up the Mexican takeout, smelled it, and looked up at me.

A lump the size of a mechanical bull crawled into my throat, and it got twenty degrees hotter in that hallway.

"My lunch," I said.

He was fidgeting with the knot on top of the bag when a door to a side room opened and an older guard stepped out, still zipping up his navy blue slacks. I checked the laminated ID pinned above the left breast pocket of his neatly pressed shirt. Gerry Hopkins.

"Thanks, John. I'm all good now. Too much coffee this morning."

John nodded, stepped out from behind the table, and disappeared through the same door Gerry had just closed.

"I'm glad to see you, Gerry," I said, staring at the briefcase.

"I bet." Gerry pointed to the sign on the wall behind him.

You are not permitted to bring these items into this facility: Mobile phones, cameras, video cameras, cigarettes, tobacco, drugs, weapons, tattooing materials, lighters, matches, glass bottles, food or drink.

Gerry picked up a pen from the table and tapped the sign next to *food or drink.*

"Sorry," I said.

He tossed the white bag into the garbage can next to him, carefully reorganized all of the other items inside the briefcase, and handed it back to me.

I was curious how Gerry could take possession of God knows how much heroin in full view of a security camera. He just tossed it in the garbage can. That was the drop. Either he or an accomplice would probably mark the trash bag, drop into the garbage bin and wait for someone else to come by and lift it. Who knows how many people were in the supply chain.

The bull in my throat was gone.

"Carolyn," shouted Gerry. "Where's this young man headed?"

"Sontag," she shouted back. "Room seven."

"Follow me, sir," said Gerry.

I followed him to a door at the end of the hallway directly below the security camera. He removed a set of keys from his front pocket and unlocked and opened the door. He ushered me through the door to another guard.

"Sontag, room seven," said Gerry.

The other guard nodded and told me to follow him. About thirty steps later, he unlocked another door and led me into a small interview room. In the middle of the room was a table about six feet long. On each side of the table sat three chairs evenly spaced apart. A whiteboard hung on one wall. Two video cameras mounted in opposite corners monitored the room.

"Have a seat," said the guard. "He'll be here in a minute."

· · ·

I HEARD Sontag before I saw him. His leg shackles clanked down the hall like some Dickensian ghost. The silver doorknob turned and a guard escorted Sontag into the room.

Even in his seventies, my old boss looked as intimidating as ever. He was balding now, and what hair he had left had turned white. He was still a solid man, with hands the size of Easter hams. He wore a white T-shirt underneath a tan short-sleeved button-up shirt, tan sweatpants, white socks, and tan slippers. From the faded tattoos that ran up both forearms, you'd think he'd been in prison for decades, but as far as I knew, this was the only time he'd been behind bars.

"This way, Joseph," said the guard, who led Sontag to the table and pulled out one of the chairs.

Sontag sat down slowly and held his arms out in front of him. He didn't speak, but stared through me as if I owed him six figures and was late on payments. The guard unlocked one of Sontag's wrists, ran the restraint behind the chair and then snapped his wrist back in the cuff. The shackle clicked as the guard ratcheted the lock tight around his wrist.

"Sorry about the irons, Joseph," said the guard. "Rules is rules."

Sontag nodded, not breaking his gaze at me.

The guard left the room and closed the door behind him. Sontag still stared at me, looming over the conference table as if it were a piece of furniture in a child's playroom.

AS FAR AS CRIMINALS GO, Joseph Sontag was as violent as they come. He started up through the ranks in his early twenties working for the Rosenthal Clan as a bagman, collecting racket payments and running errands. A few years later, Rosenthal made him a soldier and put him in charge of overseeing the narcotics business in Brooklyn's Bedford-Stuyvesant neighborhood. That's where he made the reputation that still shadowed him today.

In the 1970s, selling heroin and crack cocaine replaced the rackets, gambling, and prostitution as the mob's main money-making operation. Drugs brought in more money than all those other activities combined, but unlike those other lines of business, narcotics required a complex distribution network—a sophisticated pipeline to get product from the manufacturing centers to the street.

Rosenthal set up this New York supply through one man, a Columbian they called The Buffalo. The demand for narcotics in Bed-Stuy grew larger than anyone expected, and Rosenthal was making millions. The Buffalo, seeing how profitable the narcotics trade had become in Brooklyn, took it upon himself to renegotiate his contract, doubling Rosenthal's costs. When Rosenthal refused to pay, The Buffalo shut down the pipeline. As the supply dried up, Rosenthal's customers started going elsewhere for product, into neighborhoods controlled by Rosenthal's competition. Rosenthal knew he had to do something to reopen the supply line and sent Sontag to negotiate with The Buffalo.

No one knows exactly what happened when Sontag sat down with the Columbian because he went alone. What is known is that when Sontag walked into that warehouse in Hoboken, New Jersey, The Buffalo had two hands. When Sontag left, he only had one. Sontag had also renegotiated a new contract with The Buffalo, one that lowered Rosenthal's costs by twenty-five percent.

Sontag's management style earned him the nickname The Money Getter.

Within a year, Sontag was a lieutenant running a dozen crews and generating tens of millions for the Rosenthal Clan. Two years later, Sontag saw another opportunity. Not content with running a quarter of Rosenthal's operation, he decided to make a move.

It was a rainy Monday morning when Sontag met Rosenthal at the Black Sheep Cafe for their weekly breakfast meeting. During that meeting, Sontag told Rosenthal he was taking over the operation, and if Rosenthal didn't agree to turn over the reins and retire, he'd be dead before nightfall.

What Rosenthal didn't know was that Sontag already had the backing of the other lieutenants. The Money Getter had shared his expansion plans and convinced them they'd make more green under his leadership than with Rosenthal. Unlike with The Buffalo, Rosenthal didn't need to be persuaded to take the offer. He retired to Florida, where he died of natural causes a decade later.

And those grand expansion plans Sontag promised his clan? He delivered in spades. Within two years of taking over the top spot, the Sontag Clan had quadrupled its territory in New York, and Sontag enjoyed a forty-year reign as the most ruthless organized crime boss the city had ever seen.

That was then. Now, according to the white patch on Sontag's tan shirt, he was merely Prisoner #1053.

SONTAG LEANED FORWARD AS FAR as his restraints would allow. "Are you here to make a go at me? I'm not going to make it easy."

"I'm not here to kill you."

"Well, you sure as shit aren't part of my legal team. Why are you here, Connor?"

"Three days ago someone came into my home and tried to kill me. Alfie O'Bannon said someone from the Sontag Clan called in the hit."

"And you believed him?"

"I had a gun to his head. He didn't have cause to lie."

Sontag didn't say anything.

"Did you order it?"

"You give me a reason to send a man after you?"

"I don't know. Maybe you're tying up loose ends with your trial coming up."

"Are you a loose end, Connor?"

"No."

"You talk to anyone about me? What you used to do for me? About your time in New York?"

"No."

"Then I got no reason to send a man after you." He smiled for the first time since entering the conference room. "Besides, if I was going to come after you, I wouldn't go through Alfie O'Bannon. I'd send Porter to do it right. Blow you in half with a shotgun, and we wouldn't be having this conversation."

"What about someone else in your organization?"

"You suggesting I don't have control over my own people?"

"I've heard things. That with you on the inside, someone's making a play for your job. Maybe they're taking out anyone who might stand in their way. Anyone they perceive to be a threat."

"You've been talking to my people then."

"I'm trying to get to the bottom of who tried to kill me, so yeah, I've been talking to your people."

"You heard about Nicky? About the bomb?"

"I heard that. That's why I'm thinking someone on the inside is taking out threats. Making a clear a path for themselves."

"Probably." He sat back in his chair, the shackles dancing on the table in front of him. The gears were turning in his head, and I could tell he was trying to piece together a plan. "I need you to do something for me."

"I'm not here to get back in the game, Joseph. I just want to know who came after me."

"I need you to find Nicky. He disappeared after the attempt on his life."

"I'm not here to find Nicky. Or do any favors. I'm just here for me."

He slammed his hands on the table, snapping off a piece of particle board about six-inches long. We both looked at it recognizing the sharp, knifelike edge. I reached for it, but Sontag flicked it away with his hand. It slid across the floor, stopping in the corner of the room.

"You'll do this for me, Connor. You owe me."

"How do you figure?"

"Because when you lobbied for retirement, I cast the tie-breaking vote that kept you alive. If it wasn't for me, Porter would have splattered your gray matter all over that dining room wall. So here's what's gonna happen. You're gonna find Nicky and get him to a meeting. I'll have Messner schedule a sit-down with Spiro and Napoli. Nicky'll meet with them, and with my blessing, establish himself as the head of the Sontag

Clan. And because I sanctioned the transition, the heads of the other clans will have to abide."

"How is that going to stop whoever is trying to take over your crew?"

"They're only trying to take it over because they see me as ineffective, and they're right. There isn't much I can do from in here. The Spiro and Napoli clans are just waiting. They won't get involved until a new leader rises to the top. But if I put Nicky in that spot, they'll help him root out whoever is trying to take things over and put a stop to it."

"Why would they do that? What allegiance do they have to Nicky?"

"Because no one likes chaos, Connor. We all want things running smoothly because that's how we make money. Hiccups like this draw too much attention and threaten all of us. Spiro and Napoli are already going to be on edge with me on the inside, probably thinking they could be the feds' next target. Nicky takes the reins, and with their help, he can reestablish some form of order. Get back to normalcy. Everyone else will fall in line under him. That's how this shit works."

Sontag's logic was sound. With him in federal custody, there was a leadership vacuum in his organization, and the heads of the other families, if they stuck to the code, would stay out of things until the dust settled and a new leader was in charge. How that leader got into power wasn't their concern. There's a hierarchy in the mob, and most of what the movies portray is inaccurate. When the clans are at peace, everyone is making money hand over fist, and that's the way they like it. If something upsets that balance, it can lead to bad things.

Even though Sontag was out of commission, he was still the ruling head of the organization, and the other clans would respect that until it was proven he could no longer lead. Since he hadn't gone to trial yet and there was still a chance, albeit a slim one, that Sontag could get back out on the street, they would abide by his position. But if Sontag went to prison for a stretch and there was no one sitting on the Sontag throne, the code goes out the window and you get a turf war, which even though it could serve as a means for the other clans to expand their territory, isn't a good situation. It disrupts the status quo and shit goes downhill fast. People die and the police take notice.

If Sontag could officially install Nicky as the head of the clan, then the other families would support him, and more importantly, they wouldn't back any rogue element in Nicky's organization trying to start a coup. Whoever was behind the takeover would recognize this too and back off, effectively righting the ship and returning operations to normal. It was an ambitious plan, but it had one massive hole.

"Even if that works," I said, "it all hinges on me finding Nicky."

"Then go find him. That's what I pay you for, to do the shit that can't be done."

"You seem to be forgetting I don't work for you anymore."

"And you're failing to see how you're connected to all this. If you're right and someone in my organization came after you, then Nicky is the key to making it go away. He takes control of the clan, restores order, and your little problem disappears. It's one thing to mount a takeover with me waiting for trial, but overthrowing Nicky once he's in power, the other clans won't stand for it. No one inside this organization will be able to move on Nicky without the heads of the other families giving them permission. And they won't give permission because they want peace and order.

"But if you don't find him, or if the rogue finds him before you do and puts a bullet in his head, then it doesn't matter. We're all dead. With Nicky in place, all the extracurriculars cease, things go back to normal, and you get to keep breathing. Everybody wins."

Sontag was playing me. He wanted me to find Nicky and was pushing the right buttons to convince me why I should help him. The last thing I wanted to do was get involved in somebody else's problem, but Sontag was right. This was all connected, and to solve my problem, I had to solve his problem. And that meant I'd be back in the NYC underworld.

"Messner will be here soon and I'll tell him to put Spiro and Napoli on alert. As soon as you find Nicky, you call Messner and have him set up the meeting. Then you get Nicky to the sit-down and this all goes away."

Something told me this picture wasn't as smooth as Sontag painted it.

"Any idea where to start with Nicky?" I said.

"No idea. He almost sat on a bomb. Could be anywhere."

"You think he's still in New York?"

"I don't think he's gone far, but he won't be staying at any of the clan's safe houses. He'll be on his own, lying low until the dust settles."

I nodded and stood up, already considering the starting points for the Nicky Sontag leg of my investigation. Nicky was on my shortlist anyway, so Sontag wasn't asking me to do anything I wasn't going to do already. Sontag may be convinced his son is innocent in all this, but I still see a scenario where Nicky is behind the attempt on my life. I'd have to find him, but I'd also have to be damn cautious doing it.

Sontag's eyes burned through the back of my head as I knocked twice on the interview room door.

"Connor," said Sontag.

I turned around.

"Don't misinterpret our friendship as weakness. If you walk away from this without finding Nicky, I'll have you killed. I might not be able to do much from in here, but I can still do that."

The guard opened the door and I stepped into the hallway. I was headed toward the lobby when a familiar face stopped me.

"When I checked in, they said my colleague had already arrived," said Lyle Messner. "I thought they mixed me up with another attorney." He looked at the briefcase in my hand. "You used my name to get in here?"

"I gave you the chance to help me, and you told me to piss off."

"I think what I said was go fuck yourself."

"That's about right."

"What's to keep me from marching back there and telling them to arrest your ass for impersonating an attorney?"

"Is that a crime?"

"It is in New York state."

"You could do that, but considering your client just hired me to find his missing son and quell the hostile takeover brewing in his organization, I'd say that would be a mistake on your part."

His fist tightened around his briefcase and he turned and continued down the hall.

13

YEA OR NAY

IF YOU BELIEVE HOLLYWOOD, you'd think no one ever left organized crime. That's not true. It's difficult, and the more you know the more of a liability you are, making it harder to cut the cord. But it's still possible. I'm proof of that.

Typically, those who leave the mob retire to some warm climate and live out their days on a beach resort, like Rosenthal did when Sontag edged him out. No one thought he'd be a problem. Just like some corporate CEO, he had served his purpose and was replaced by someone the organization thought would be more effective.

My situation was different. I left Sontag's organization voluntarily. Also different was, unlike Sontag's other associates, I wasn't an official member of the clan. I was more of a designated hitter, brought in when they needed me and riding the bench otherwise. I did project work, but my part-time status didn't exclude me from one of three scenarios that awaited if I continued with this lifestyle. One, I do something to piss off someone who had Sontag's ear, or even Sontag himself, and they turn on me. Two, a rival organization takes an interest in not wanting me around anymore and uses some painful means to remove me from the NYC crime scene. Or three, the feds or NYPD pick me up for services completed on Sontag's behalf and lock me away in a cage for forty years. Old, alive, and free are mutually exclusive in this business.

I was having lunch with Sontag at his favorite restaurant when I mentioned I might be thinking of retiring. I didn't plan to broach the topic right then and there over a meatloaf sandwich and jalapeño potato chips, it just happened. It wasn't an official declaration of my intent to retire, either. I was more floating a trial balloon to see his reaction. I didn't expect the silence that followed. Then he quickly changed the subject.

I'd forgotten I even brought it up when a week later a black town car screeched to a stop in front of my apartment as I returned from a morning coffee run.

Nitty Ford, Sontag's bodyman and primary driver, was behind the wheel. Porter rolled down the rear window. "Get in, Connor. We got a meeting." He opened the door and I climbed inside.

Nitty drove us to Sontag's beach house in Greenwich, Connecticut, an hour away from his Upper East Side headquarters. The home was in an exclusive neighborhood overlooking Long Island Sound. From the outside, the place looked like it belonged on the cover of some New England life magazine, but the inside was practically empty, except for a dining room table and a few chairs. The kitchen didn't even have a refrigerator. It wasn't meant for comfort, only business. I'd met Sontag there maybe a dozen times over the years. It was a clean site— a professional crew routinely swept the place for bugs—and it's where Sontag conducted his most sensitive business. Whatever we were going to discuss was going to be big.

We arrived at the beach house around eleven in the morning. It wasn't until I stepped out of the car and Porter demanded my weapon that I realized what was going on. I assumed we were going to discuss another assignment, but I didn't know I was on the agenda. I was wrong when I thought Sontag had ignored me when I brought up retirement. He hadn't. He merely tabled the conversation for a week.

I relinquished my .45 to Porter and he walked me past a black Mercedes-Benz E-Class station wagon to the front door.

Three knocks and we were in the foyer.

"They're waiting for you in the dining room," said Porter. "However this plays out, we're going to miss you."

"What are you talking about?" I asked.

"Your retirement."

I didn't say anything.

"You can't talk about leaving and expect Sontag to just let it go," said Porter. "He's gonna question your loyalty." He extended his arm and, looking a bit like the Grim Reaper, pointed his finger down the hall to the dining room.

I hesitated for a moment, preparing myself for what waited in the other room.

"Now," said Porter.

I moved forward, thinking with each step that I was marching toward my death. But then I remembered what Porter had said. *However this plays out.* That meant there were options. I picked up my pace, feeling Porter looming behind me.

In the dining room, Sontag, Nicky, and Franklin Bockhold, Sontag's advisor, sat drinking coffee at the polished walnut dining table. Their relaxed demeanor suggested they'd be discussing which landscaper to hire, not whether I lived or died.

Sontag motioned me toward the chair placed in front of the table. I approached and sat down.

"You still want out?" asked Sontag.

"It was just a conversation," I said, remembering our chat over lunch a week earlier. "I hadn't really made a decision."

"But you were thinking it. Why?"

I didn't have a specific reason to give Sontag. Aside from not wanting to spend the rest of my life dead or in prison, I didn't see myself working for the mob forever. Of course, I didn't have any other irons in the fire. I was a retired Army intelligence officer, which didn't really have many practical applications outside of law enforcement, which given my underworld occupation for the past six years, was out of the question. I had nothing lined up and wasn't sure where I wanted to go. I just knew running with Sontag's clan was never a permanent situation, and it wasn't something I wanted to define my life when I looked back on it in forty-plus years. So I gave him the only story that came to mind.

"My father is sick," I said. "Prostate cancer."

"How advanced is it?" asked Sontag.

"Stage three."

"So, he's got a shot."

"He's got a shot, but we're talking hospital visits and tests for the next God knows how long."

Sontag pressed. "Where is he?"

"Boston."

"And that's where you're headed?"

"Guess so."

"How long have you been thinking about leaving?"

"I hadn't really put a ton of thought in it until now. My father just told me about the diagnosis. He's been undergoing tests for the last month, so I didn't really have a reason to mention it."

It wasn't complete bullshit. Albert was sick, but he made it damn clear that he didn't want either of his boys upending their lives over his prostate. Still, it was the best excuse I had to give Sontag.

"Here's how this works, "said Sontag. "The three of us have a chat and decide if we think you're a good fit for retirement or not."

He didn't have to explain what happens if they decided not to grant me a release. There was a reason Porter took my weapon.

I nodded and the three men stood up and left the room. They marched out in single file like a jury going to deliberate a verdict.

That's when I heard the familiar click of my .45's hammer locking. I slowly turned around to find Porter leveling my own weapon at my head.

"What did I just walk into?" I asked.

"A vote. If they come back in your favor, you walk out of here. Otherwise, you don't." He made a spiral-motion with the weapon. "Turn back around."

I've been shot at too many times to count, but this was the first time I'd ever had a weapon pointed at my head execution style. It's difficult to describe how that feels, other than everything in your body tightens and you feel like you have to use the bathroom. And it gets cold. Teeth-chattering cold. That whole thing about life flashing in front of you is true, but it's not in some chronological order. It's sporadic, like a dream, and sometimes it doesn't make any sense, like your noggin is screwing with you.

I thought about Albert and my brother, Finn. I had a vivid flashback about a summer at our family lake house in Maine. I was just a kid then, and the memory threw me. There wasn't anything remarkable about it. It wasn't a moment that should appear on my life's highlight reel, but there it was nonetheless. All three of us were fishing from the dock, and then my mother called down from the house that lunch was ready. Our boat, a sleek wooden thing tied to the end of the dock, bobbed in the gentle waves. A moment later, I was maybe five or six years old, standing next to my mother at a department store that was going out of business. We were pulling a four-foot tall teddy bear off the shelf. It was marked down seventy percent. Everything must go.

The memory faded and I found myself laughing out loud that the last things that might go through my brain, aside from a .45 slug, were memories of fishing and getting a teddy bear at a ridiculous discount. Profound stuff.

My mind left the memories behind and instead focused on the irony of the situation. Back in the Army, I used several interrogation methods, including some that might seem barbaric, to extract information from detainees. I thought back to the last person I interrogated. I tied his hands behind his back, knelt him down facing a corner, and placed my weapon to the back of his head. I cocked the hammer, which was loud in such a small room, and through a translator told him I was prepared to kill him then and there if he didn't give me the information I wanted. The psychological effects of interrogation are paralyzing, but they're also effective. He told us what we needed to know, and I assumed it resulted in American lives being saved. At least that's what I've always told myself. That detainee didn't know it, of course, but I had no intention of killing him, even if he didn't give us what we wanted. The carefully orchestrated exercise was just an extreme method to get him to talk. Porter, on the other hand, wouldn't hesitate to blow my head clean off if things didn't come back in my favor.

"How long's this going to take? I can't imagine having a gun pointed at my head is good for my mental state."

"They'll be back when they're ready. Try not to think about it."

What seemed like another ten minutes passed, and the inside of my head fell still and dark, like a movie theater after everyone went home and the sixteen-year-old with bad acne had mopped up the popcorn and spilled Coke. I waited for more memories to come, memories of my family or my time in the Army, but my synapses were tapped out.

Then, the three-person commission returned. I took that as a good sign. Had their decision been a "no," I assumed they would have just signaled Porter to put me down from the hallway. Why risk getting covered in blood splatter by standing too close to me?

Sontag motioned to Porter, who pocketed the weapon. The feeling of immense terror of having a gun pointed at your head is only eclipsed by the bowel-releasing relief of seeing it lowered.

My boss leaned over the table. "Thanks for your service, Connor." He shook my hand with a grip strong enough to break my fingers. "We've discussed it, and we've decided to approve your request to leave our organization. No strings attached. The terms of our decision include the following. After this conversation, Nitty will drive you to your apartment.

You'll have some time to gather your belongings and then we expect you to leave New York. You're not to return. You're not to have contact with anyone in our organization or our associates. You're free to do whatever the hell you want as long as it doesn't interfere with our interests. Violation of these terms will mean the dissolution of our verbal agreement, and things will go bad for you very quickly. Do you agree with these terms?"

"I agree with your terms," I said, sounding much too formal. "And thanks."

"Don't mention it," said Sontag. Then he smiled. "To anyone."

"I won't."

"This will be the last conversation you and I will ever have."

"Understood."

"And I hope things work out with your father in Boston."

"Thanks. Me too."

Porter handed my .45 back to me. "Let's go." He led me to the town car. He and Nitty escorted me to my apartment, where they watched me pack everything I owned into my green Army duffle and a dented metal suitcase. An hour later I was on I-91 headed to Boston with a clean slate.

14

ROUTINES AND REDHEADS

THERE WASN'T much consistency in New York organized crime. Keeping a routine was a guaranteed way to get into trouble. That's why most everyone in Sontag's organization went out of their way to avoid setting a schedule. They never met with the same people at the same times, and never went to the same places on the same day. That unwritten rule didn't apply to Gretchen Sontag, Joseph's wife, who every Tuesday had brunch at the Palm Court in the Plaza Hotel. Like clockwork, she'd arrive at ten in the morning, enjoy brunch, and then spend the rest of the day in the hotel's spa. She always ate alone at the same table overlooking Central Park. The same schedule every Tuesday.

I had zero leads on Nicky Sontag. I hoped Gretchen could remedy that.

The Plaza was buzzing when I arrived. Guests in more expensive attire than my borrowed suit crisscrossed the lobby's white and gold marble floor. I moved through the crowd, passing cherubs on pedestals and vases overflowing with purple flowers. A crystal chandelier the size of a Volkswagen

Beetle hung overhead. I never liked the Plaza. Its opulence made me nervous to touch anything. Even in my mid-forties, I felt like a kid in an antique store.

When I arrived at the entrance to the Palm Court restaurant, a hostess in a long, sleek navy blue dress approached, but I brushed her off. "I'm meeting someone, thanks."

Across the room, at her usual table, Gretchen sat sipping a thin flute of champagne. She wore a black silk blazer over a low-cut beige top. Her skirt was short enough that only its edge was visible under her jacket. At fifty-seven, she still turned a lot of heads. She sat alone, but everyone in the restaurant knew she was there.

I walked over and sat down without asking for permission.

"Well, look who it is," she said, taking a long, slow sip. "Back from the dead."

"Not dead, retired."

"Same thing." She ran an elegant finger around the rim of her plate. "What in the hell are you doing here? If I remember correctly, you're not a fan of brunch. Why was that again?"

"I think it's pretentious. Something people do just to say they do it. Like yoga. It's also lazy. I've got too much shit to do to wait until ten a.m. to eat something."

"I'm sure the chef would disagree." She bit into a strawberry. "How long have you been back?"

"Not long."

"Well, it's good to see you. Really good."

A bald waiter in a white jacket, black slacks, and a brass name tag approached the table. "Will the gentleman be enjoying brunch with you this morning, ma'am?"

"I don't know, Roberto." She dropped the strawberry on her plate. "Mr. Harding simply detests brunch. But perhaps we can persuade him to step out of his comfort zone." She took another sip of champagne. "What do you think, Mr. Harding?"

"Just coffee," I said.

"Yes, sir." The waiter shot me an awkward glance, placed his hands behind his back, and walked away.

"See, that's what I'm talking about," I said. "That look he gave me. As if I'm not good enough to eat brunch at The Plaza. Pretentious."

"No, he gave you that look because your suit jacket is two sizes too small. I'd tell you to fire your tailor, but we both know you don't have one."

"I don't, and this isn't even my suit."

"Why are you wearing someone else's... You know what, never mind. I don't want to know. Where have you been for the past two years?"

"Boston."

"And what brings you back?"

"I'm looking for Nicky. You know where I might be able to find him?"

"No. I assume you should check with your old colleagues."

"Already did that. Even talked to your husband a half hour ago. Nicky's AWOL, and it's important I find him."

The waiter returned with a silver tray. He set a ceramic cup and saucer in front of me, raised the carafe high into the air and poured the coffee like it was some sort of show.

"A lot of trouble for a cup of coffee," I said.

"Don't worry, Roberto," said Gretchen. "Mr. Harding doesn't appreciate panache. He prefers his coffee in paper cups."

Roberto offered a quick nod, turned and left with the tray.

"I don't know where Nicky is," she said.

"You don't seem too worried about him."

"Why should I? He's not *my* kid. Let Joseph worry about him."

"He is worried about him. That's why I'm sitting here in an ill-fitting suit drinking a twenty-seven dollar cup of coffee."

"Well, I can't help you, Connor." She sucked on another strawberry. "But I'd be careful if you do go out looking for him. Nicky's not going to want to see you.

"Why's that?"

"Nicky never liked you. Maybe it's your shitty disposition. Or maybe he thinks you helped put Joseph away."

"Why would he think that?"

"After they picked Joseph up, Nicky was paranoid they had tapped the phones uptown, so he spent the day at my place making calls. I don't know who he was talking to, but I heard Nicky running down a list of names he thought may be involved in Joseph's arrest."

"And my name came up?"

"Yes. So if you do find Nicky, know that he might be looking for you too."

Every time I began to think Nicky wasn't behind Boston, something like this tried to convince me otherwise.

"Thanks for the concern, Gretch. Are you still tied into things around here? Things happening in the organization?"

"What, are you wearing a wire or something?"

"No. I wouldn't be able to hide it underneath this tight suit anyway."

She smiled. "What specifically do you want to know?"

"I hear Nicky's car bomb was part of a power grab. With Sontag away, someone's trying to take over the organization. They want Nicky out."

"How do you know Nicky wasn't the one who orchestrated the power grab? And that the car bomb was someone else retaliating for something Nicky did?"

"Is that what happened?"

"I don't know any specifics about the bomb, but I do know Nicky was upset Joseph didn't transfer power when the feds picked him up. Nicky felt he was due."

"If it's any consolation, Joseph changed his mind. That's why I'm looking for Nicky. Joseph plans on anointing him chief to quell an uprising.

She slid her champagne flute aside and leaned in. "Is that right?"

"You sure you don't have any information on where I can find him?"

"No. I really have no idea where he is. Maybe Victor could help."

"Why's that?"

"Because Victor knows a hell of a lot more than I do about what's happing inside the organization. Why the hesitation? Does he hate you too?"

"Don't know, but he's on my shortlist of people who might want me dead."

"Why would Victor want you dead?"

"That's not a story I'm ready to get into right now."

"Suit yourself, but if you're looking for Nicky, I'd start there."

I blew across the top of my coffee and took a sip. I had to admit, it was pretty good. "If you hear anything, will you let me know?"

"Sure, but don't count on it. I've been living here at the

hotel for the past month, and these days I don't cross paths with anyone you'd be interested in."

"Why are you staying here?"

"No reason to be at that big house all by myself."

She sipped more champagne. Her heavy gold bracelet slid up and down her thin forearm each time she raised her glass.

"Come on, Connor. You know he's never getting out of prison. There's nothing here for me anymore." She brushed her dark red hair behind her ear, revealing a diamond stud earring the size of an M&M. "Want a tour of my suite? I could get you out of that horrendous suit for a spell. For old times' sake."

Normally, I would have jumped at the chance, but something didn't feel right. Maybe it was because Sontag was rotting away waiting for trial, or because I knew there was someone out there who still wanted me dead.

"It's tempting, but I've got a lot of stones to turn over."

"Maybe another time," she said. "You know where to find me. Where can I find you?"

"The Beacon." I stood up and set my coffee cup on the saucer.

"Did you ever tell Joseph about us?" I asked.

"Of course not. That would be suicide for both of us. Why do you ask?"

"There seems to be a growing number of people who want to kill me. Just curious if I should keep Joseph on that list."

"Nicky wouldn't miss any opportunity to piss on your shoes, but Joseph... He always liked you. That's probably why Nicky didn't."

"It was good to see you again, Gretch. Maybe we'll cross paths again."

"I hope so." She tilted her head back and finished her

champagne. "That list you're working on. I hope it's not a very long one."

"It's longer than I'd like it to be."

She winked.

I walked back toward the lobby.

15

GREENWICH, CONNECTICUT

FINDING an asset who doesn't want to be found is an art form, and for the most part, it's easy. People leave footprints everywhere, and all it takes is to apply the right strategy from the detailed checklist in my head. It starts, as most investigations do, with a phone call.

I didn't have Nicky's cell, but Porter would, so I called him. It didn't take me long to convince him I was working for Sontag and needed to find Nicky before someone else did. Porter was happy to provide the digits. I dialed, and for a moment I thought Nicky might answer. That would be too easy. Of course, even if he did answer, there wasn't anything I could say to lure him out of hiding. As far as he knew, I was the person coming after him, and no matter what I told him over the phone, he wasn't going to pop his head up and let someone take a shot. I waited anyway, counting the rings. After ten rings, he didn't pick up and there was no option to leave a message, so I hung up. On to step two.

These days, most everyone is on some social media

website. It's the easiest way to find someone. Most criminals are stupid. It's why they're criminals. We've all heard of the bank robber who wrote the give-me-the-money note to the bank teller on the back of his dry cleaning receipt. Social media also has its equal share of morons. I can't count the number of times I've heard of someone on the run posting a photo to a website, leading the authorities right to them. Nicky wasn't your average criminal, and while he's prone to make mistakes, he wouldn't make that one. Except for his cell phone, he stayed as far away from technology and the Internet as he could. He didn't even have an email address because it was too easy to track. He handled all of his business in person, something he learned from his old man.

Past employers are another great way to find someone. Even people on the run often file an address with their previous employers to get any future paychecks. I've found three people over the years by merely calling their employer and claiming I was an insurance investigator following up on a workers' comp claim. Employers love to rat out anyone they think is running an insurance fraud scheme. That approach wouldn't work for Nicky either, as the Sontag Clan had no HR department.

My next option was to find a connector, someone who knows the asset and can lead me right to them. Maybe someone who doesn't even know the asset is in hiding. Parents, ex-girlfriends, college buddies, coworkers, anyone who could have an address, alternate phone number, or something. This was a dangerous approach because I didn't know who inside the Sontag Clan was still loyal to Nicky. I assumed Porter was, but he didn't know where Nicky was hiding out, or if he did know, I'd been unable to convince him to give him up.

If I asked the wrong person, I could end up with a baseball bat to the back of my head, something I wasn't about to entertain.

Nicky wasn't your typical mark and the usual approach wasn't going to work. I started with what I knew. From my time in New York, I knew the Sontag Clan had a dozen or more safe houses throughout the five boroughs. Places that were off the beaten path where one could cool off if the heat got too intense. I used the house in Brooklyn twice when I had to disappear for a few weeks.

Nicky wouldn't hole up in any of the safe houses though. If whoever was after him was on the inside, they'd know all the same rabbit holes Nicky did. It was too risky. Nicky would have to go deep underground, and in this city, that could be anywhere.

Nicky had a home in Tribeca, at least he did the last time I was here. That would be a safe place to hold out for a while, but not long term. Whoever was after him would station a man or two on the outside and wait for Nicky to come out for food or some other necessity to go in. Once they had proof their target was inside, they'd go in firing in all directions until they hit something. Or they'd station a sniper on the neighboring rooftop and pop Nicky through a window.

Nicky would need to acquire another residence outside the city. The beach house where Porter once held a gun to my head was a logical starting point. Only a few high-ranking members of the clan knew about it, and Sontag went to great lengths to keep it that way. Sontag used the residence for highly sensitive meetings, the kind of meetings Nicky and I were usually involved in. The beach house was a good place to look. Nicky would want to stay close to the city in case he needed to step back into his role, and the beach house was only an hour away. That was my first stop.

I FOLLOWED I-95 TO GREENWICH. Sontag's beach house was behind a solid iron wall about seven feet high. From outside the wall, it was impossible to see if any vehicles were in the driveway. Parking in front of the property and buzzing the intercom wasn't going to cut it, so I drove a half mile up the street, parked in a convenience store lot, and strolled back toward the house via the sandy beach. The houses were far apart, privacy the owners paid a hefty price tag for. The wind blew across Long Island Sound and cut into me. I pulled my jacket up around my neck and watched as the surf crashed along the beach.

Aside from a photographer shooting toward the water and a couple holding hands and struggling to conquer the sand, cold, and wind, the beach was deserted. I kept close to the tall grass on the high-end of the beach to stay concealed from anyone who might be watching the area from Sontag's home. I doubted Nicky would have an extensive security detail protecting him, but all it took was one person inside that house to take an interest in the man in the green military jacket coming down the beach to screw things up.

I was just about to come upon the house when an older couple walking a black-and-white beagle stepped onto the sand and stopped directly behind Sontag's home, about twenty yards from where I was going to hop the wall. They laughed, plastic bag in hand, as their beagle squatted on the sand. I walked past them, fighting the urge to look up at the house. If there was someone up there, I didn't want to draw any attention to myself.

I slowed down, passed the house and waited for the couple and their mutt to move along. After a moment, they did. I looked over my shoulder and lingered until they were far enough away they wouldn't hear what I did next. Satisfied, I took another glance around the beach, and not seeing anyone, I ran full speed toward the Great Wall of Sontag, leaped out of the sand, grabbed the top of the wall and boosted myself over to the other side. I was up and over in less than three seconds, and when I landed, I scrambled across the small back yard until I reached the back of the house.

Sontag's beach house was a two-story stone structure that resembled an old English manor. There was a wooden staircase that led to a wooden deck overlooking the sound that spanned the entire width of the back of the house. There were two sets of doors leading from the living room to the back deck, flanked by several windows. If there was anyone in the living room, they'd see me the moment I ascended the steps onto the porch. On the side of the house though, were two basement windows. I knew from my previous trips to the home that an alarm company monitored the place, but I remembered the alarm keypad next to the front door was an older unit, which meant the alarm window sensors were probably old too.

Windows are the weak point of most security systems. The alarm company installs sensors on the window frame and the wall just above the frame. As long as those two sensors are touching, the alarm doesn't trip. The trouble comes when you open the window, which breaks the circuit between the two sides of the sensor. The result is a screeching siren and a police visit. Bypassing the alarm is as simple as breaking the window, but keeping the frame intact.

Hi-tech alarm systems include vibration monitors and glass-break sensors which can trip an alarm should someone break the glass, like I was about to do, but as I said, Sontag had an older system. I dropped to the ground and laid on my side next to a basement window. Thanks to the imposing wall surrounding the home, there was no chance anyone would see me. I drew my right leg up and drove my boot through the glass, shattering it into big chunks, which fell to the concrete floor inside the home. No alarm siren. I used my boot heel to chip away the remaining bits of glass from the window frame, and when it was clear, I climbed through, landing on the concrete floor.

I drew my .45 and climbed the steps to the main level. I opened the basement door, but before I entered the kitchen, I scanned the walls for motion sensors. Nothing. I couldn't remember if Sontag had motion sensors or not, but even if there were, they wouldn't be turned on if someone was inside the house. You usually only activate those at night or when you've left home. If Nicky were hiding out here, they'd likely be turned off.

Crossing the kitchen floor, I listened for any signs that someone was in the house. Talking, television, anything. The home was silent, and it had a musty smell as if the windows and doors hadn't been opened for a while. I reached the entrance to the living room and slowly peered around the corner. The room was bare. No furniture or any other signs someone was here. There was a motion sensor on the far wall, which meant I'd have to bypass that to get to the steps to make it to the upper level. The home had four bedrooms on the second level, so if Nicky were staying here, there would be some sign upstairs, something as simple as a toothbrush in the bathroom. If I found anything, I'd wait for him to return. But first, I'd have to get upstairs.

Motion sensors are easy to fool if you know how. Most beam motion sensors, the type common in home security systems, don't cover the entire field of view. They have blind spots. The best way to defeat them is to walk slowly against the wall underneath the motion sensor. That's their weak point. The sensor I was looking at was on the other side of the wall, so getting underneath it wasn't going to happen. The other option is to stay low to the floor. Most people have pets, which is why motion sensors aren't calibrated to scan the floor. The last thing a homeowner wants is for Whiskers to trip the motion sensors while roaming the house at night. There is about a twelve-to-eighteen-inch dead space along the floor.

I slipped my .45 back inside my jacket, laid on the kitchen floor and slowly crawled into the living room. I flattened my body as much as I could for a six-one, 195-pound man and Army crawled to the foot of the steps. As I moved, I listened for anyone who might be upstairs. Nothing. I made it to the base of the steps, which was along the same wall as the motion sensor, and slowly crawled up the steps, keeping my chest against the carpeting the entire way up the stairs. Reaching the top of the steps, I scanned the upstairs hallway but saw no motion sensors. I stood up, drew my weapon again and checked each bedroom.

There were no signs anyone had been in this house for months. All the beds were made and there were no personal items of any kind in the bedrooms or bathrooms. When your life is on the line, most people will do all they can to keep hidden, and that means removing all traces that you're staying somewhere, but this house was too clean. I doubted even Nicky would go to such lengths to conceal his living here. There was one more telling sign. I checked the two upstairs bathrooms and found red rings around the water line in the toilets. No one had flushed them in weeks. You can cover your tracks as much as possible, but everyone has to piss.

Sontag's Greenwich beach house was a bust, but it was a good first stop on my investigation. I walked back to the top of the steps, laid back down on the floor, and crawled back to the kitchen. A few minutes later, I was climbing out through the shattered basement window. Since there wasn't anyone in the home, I decided to abandon the wall climb and instead strolled down the driveway and left the property through a tall gate in the security wall.

The silver SUV parked down the street caught my eye immediately. It hadn't been there when I first drove past the house some forty-five minutes ago. At this distance, I couldn't tell the make for sure, but I was leaning toward a Toyota High-lander. I checked behind me after walking three hundred feet to see if it was still there, and it was. I didn't see it again until I reached the convenience store parking lot and opened my car door. It rolled past much faster than the posted twenty-five-miles-per-hour limit. Confirmed Toyota Highlander. It was impossible to tell if it was the same SUV parked outside the beach house, and even if it was the same vehicle, it didn't necessarily mean anything. Maybe the driver pulled over to find driving directions on his phone. Probably best not to over-think it.

I drove past the beach house on my way back to New York City and the SUV was gone.

Don't overthink it.

16

BRICK HENRY

REMEMBER when I said one method of finding someone is to look at the those around them, the connectors? Nicky didn't have many connectors. His father was in federal custody, and he didn't have a woman as far as I knew. But he did have Brick Henry. Brick had been Nicky's bodyguard for as long as I could remember. He was attached to Nicky's side like a 245-pound belt loop. If anyone was still loyal to Nicky, it was Brick.

Lucky for me, Brick was married, and while I had no idea where he and Nicky were, I had a good idea where his wife was—their brownstone in Brooklyn's Bed-Stuy neighborhood. Brick was as tough as they came, but he had a solid brain in his head. If I could get to him, I could convince him to talk to Nicky and explain Sontag's plan. Using Brick as a go-between, Nicky might hear me out. There was no guarantee, but it was my best next step.

. . .

I ARRIVED at Brick's brownstone and knocked on the front door. An attractive woman in her forties opened it. She didn't say anything. Instead, she waited for me to speak.

"I'm a friend of Nicky Sontag's and I'm looking for Brick. Is he here?"

"No." She squinted her eyes against the afternoon sun.

"Do you know how I can reach him? It's important that I talk to him."

She eyeballed me up and down. We'd never met, and given the people Nicky and Brick associated with, she had every right to be suspicious. I'd worry if she wasn't.

After a moment, she nodded. "Come in. I can get you a number."

"Thank you."

I followed as she walked inside the house.

"Stay there," she said. "I'll be right back."

I closed the door and watched her disappear into the kitchen.

A moment later, someone rammed me from behind, sending me across the foyer and into the kitchen. I never played football, but I imagined this is what it felt like to be laid out by a linebacker. My side hit the counter next to the sink and I fell to the floor. I turned, expecting to see Brick rushing in from the foyer, but it wasn't him. Instead, someone I'd never seen before was coming at me with his right fist drawn back.

"Get him," yelled the woman who had opened the door. The big man had a wide neck and looked like he got paid to do what he was doing to me. He grabbed the counter and thrust a leather work boot into my ribs. He stomped, pulled back and stomped again, keeping his right hand on the counter for balance.

I shielded my side from each blow with my elbow. When he stopped to reposition himself, I snatched his boot and twisted at his ankle until it snapped. He tried to stand on it but collapsed to the floor. Scrambling to my feet, I reached for my weapon, but the woman hit me from behind with something heavy dropping me on top of the man with the broken ankle. My right shoulder and arm immediately fell numb.

The man underneath me rolled over and threw his left elbow into my jaw. Sitting up, he swung his right fist, but I rolled out of the way and he connected with the stainless steel refrigerator, denting it and probably shattering a few bones in his hand. I'd used the counter to climb to my feet when the woman hit me from behind again, knocking me back on top of the big man. As I fell on top of him, he slammed his right hand into my stomach, screaming as his broken hand connected with my midsection. The damage to his hand sucked a lot of juice from the punch, but it still hurt like hell.

I punched the side of his neck, then delivered a second quick strike to his jaw, snapping his head back against the tile floor. I staggered backward. Somehow, he got to his knees and seized a knife from a block on the counter. He held it out in front, still trying to balance on his ankle. I stepped aside, snatched my .45 from inside my jacket and buffaloed his wrist, snapping it. He dropped the knife and fell to the ground screaming through clenched teeth. I staggered backward and raised my weapon.

"You hurt my brother," the woman said.

"Tell him to stay down and that's as far as it goes," I said, trying to catch my breath.

"You kill us and you'll never—"

"I'm not here to kill anyone." I braced myself against the

counter with my free hand. "I'm working for Nicky's father. Nicky's in trouble and it's important I find him before anyone else does."

She knelt beside her brother and examined his hand. It bent upward at a sharp angle. She wiped her face and looked up at me.

I pocketed the .45, hoping it would encourage her to talk.

"I don't know where he is," she said.

"You Brick's wife?"

"That's right. Haven't seen him in a month."

That made sense. Brick was probably sticking close to Nicky. He wasn't likely to surface in case of an ambush. That also explained the brother. He probably moved in to protect his sister.

"I'm sorry for the tussle, but I only came here to talk. If you speak to Brick—if he calls or comes home—ask him to contact me." I swiped the small whiteboard and dry-erase marker from the refrigerator, wrote down my cell number, and handed it to Brick's wife. "Connor Harding."

"How do I know you're who you say you are?"

"Tell Brick what I told you about me working for Joseph. Give him that number and have him call me. I'll explain everything to him. I know they're underground, and I can get them out of all this, but I have to find them first."

They both stared at me with awkward glances, probably trying to figure out if I was really there to help Brick and Nicky or not.

I staggered past Brick's wife and her brother, keeping a hand inside my jacket on my weapon just in case they had another round in them. Their eyes followed me to the front door.

The feeling was returning to my right arm as I left the brownstone and went back to my Jeep. I sat in my vehicle, closed my eyes and thought about my next move. I couldn't shake the feeling the beach house was somehow connected to Nicky's whereabouts. The more I thought about that house, the more I wondered if Sontag had any other properties he kept in his back pocket, tucked away from everyone, even those closest to him.

For a career criminal, Sontag has a smart head on his shoulders. He was the type of person who would keep a property off the books just to have a place to disappear to if the need arose. A place only Nicky might know about. There was one way to find out. Time for some research.

BED-STUY'S public library was on Franklin Avenue, a few blocks away. It was a square brick building with two globe lamps flanking the main entrance like an old fashioned police station. After filling out a short form promising I wouldn't use their computers for anything illegal, they gave me a sign-in code. A few minutes later, I was accessing the auditor's website for Fairfield County, Connecticut. I plugged in the address for Sontag's beach house and scanned the property profile. It only took a few seconds to find it. A company called the Triton Partnership purchased the property in 2012. The Triton Partnership was likely a shell company Sontag set up to protect his identity. It was a good bet if Sontag bought any other properties, he purchased them using the same company.

I went back to the Fairfield County Auditor's main webpage and ran another search. This time, instead of plugging in a property address, I searched for the Triton Partnership.

Two properties. The beach house and another home on Wolver Hollow Road in Brookville, New York. I'd never heard any mention of that property. I searched for the address and found an aerial view of the property. The place looked like a compound. It was surrounded by a wall and was at least four times larger than the beach house. A perfect place to hide out. I checked the distance. It was on Long Island, only an hour-and-a-half from the library. I jotted down the address on a piece of scrap paper, stashed it in my front jeans pocket and headed for the door.

The sun was clocking out when I left the library. I'd rather scope out Sontag's newly found property in the dark anyway. It would be easier to get onto the grounds under cover of darkness, but it would also be easier to tell if anyone was living there. The beach house was deserted, and it's possible this one was too. If the place were lit up, however, at least I'd have some indication someone was there. Of course, lights could be on timers, but watching the place for a few minutes would tell me if someone was inside or not. I turned the corner and walked toward my car parked in the library's back lot.

The good feeling I carried out of the library disappeared when something cold struck me at the base of my skull. My entire body went numb, and as I staggered forward unable to keep my balance, my vision blurred. The single streetlamp in front of me became two, three, and then four white orbs of vibrating light. Then I heard a voice behind me and everything went dark.

17

AN OLD FRIEND

WHEN I CAME TO, I was in the trunk of a car and we were moving. My brain felt like a puzzle someone dropped on the floor. All the pieces were there, but they weren't in the right order. I tried to reach up and inspect the back of my head to make sure everything was still on the inside, but I couldn't move my arms. They were cinched behind me. It felt like a zip tie.

My fractured thoughts flashed back to the silver SUV that had been following me when I drove out to Sontag's beach house, but this wasn't an SUV. From the size of the trunk, I was in a mid-sized sedan. My face was pressed into the trunk's carpet, and every breath I drew in brought a flood of bleach vapor into my lungs. My nasal passages and chest burned. I had no idea how long I'd been inhaling the stuff.

My current situation was bad, but it was going to plummet when this car stopped and that trunk lid opened. There's only one reason a car smells like bleach; someone had cleaned up a mess. A biological mess. And they were likely prepared to do it again.

If I could get my hands free, I'd have a chance. Maybe I could find a tire iron or a road flare to use as a weapon, or I could simply come out swinging. But if I couldn't get out of these ties, I wouldn't be putting up much of a fight.

Zip ties and duct tape are the easiest restraints to escape. They might look intimidating, but if you know what you're doing, it doesn't take much effort to break them. All it requires is momentum. If restrained from the front, all you have to do is raise your arms above their head, bring them down with as much force as possible and pull your wrists apart when you reach your waist. The force generated will snap most restraints in two. That's tougher when restrained from behind, as you're limited to how high you can raise your arms. The maneuver still works, although it takes several attempts. Unfortunately, the trunk didn't give me much room to move. Using my right shoulder, I scooted myself as close to the trunk latch as I could, creating more space between the rear wall of the trunk and my hands. Then I curled up into the fetal position, which allowed me to get more range of motion. I lifted my hands as far back as possible and slammed them down onto my tailbone, forcing my wrists apart. My first shot didn't do anything, so I tried again and then again. With each attempt, my heart pumped faster and my lungs expanded wider to keep up. More bleach singed my insides. My throat felt like a charcoal briquette.

The inside of the trunk glowed red—the brake lights. I worked the restraints again and felt the locking mechanism give way. It didn't break, but it loosened enough I could slip my hands out. More brake lights, and then the vehicle took a right turn off the road. Did they hear me in the trunk?

The brake lights illuminated the trunk again, and I used the few seconds of brightness to scan the inside of the trunk, looking for anything I could use as a weapon. There was nothing in here except me and the bleach-soaked carpet. I ripped the carpet up from the floor, feeling around for a panel. Most cars have a spare tire compartment, which might have a jack, a tool kit or something useful in a situation like this.

The car stopped as my fingers found the handle to the spare compartment. I scooted toward the rear seat to give me more room and jerked on the cover, buckling it in two. I blindly searched the compartment as feet pounded the asphalt outside the vehicle. As my fingers raked the inside of the bin searching for anything I could use, someone else's fingers ran along the outside of the trunk looking for the release. They found what they were looking for before I did and the truck sprang open. Fresh air rushed in, overpowering the bleach fumes.

The sun had already set and I couldn't focus enough to identify the man standing over me. In the blackness of the trunk, I didn't realize how much the blow to my head—or maybe it was the lingering bleach vapors—had screwed up my vision. It wasn't until he opened his mouth that I realized why I was here.

"Alfie O'Bannon says hello."

The man above me drove two meaty fists into my gut, probably rupturing something important. Then he grabbed my arm and jerked me out of the trunk, nearly dislocating my shoulder. I fell to the ground and realized I was in a parking lot. The man I didn't recognize kicked me in the ribs.

"That's enough," said someone else. I looked back and saw the second man. He was tall and thin. The man with the fists and size-thirteen wingtips was on the heavy side. The bigger man grabbed both my wrists and dragged me across the asphalt. The other man leaned inside the car and returned with a sawed-off shotgun. A moment later, I was sitting on a beat-to-shit park bench.

The lean man pointed the shotgun at my head from six feet away while his partner pulled a smartphone from his pocket and tapped the screen. A few seconds later I was staring at Alfie O'Bannon.

"Hello, Connor. Surprised to see me?"

"Honestly, yes. I didn't think I'd have to deal with you until I got back to Boston. How's the leg?"

"Still hurts like a bitch. But I'm going to be just fine. You, on the other hand, are not."

"I gathered that. I suppose there isn't anything I can say to make you reconsider your decision here?"

"No," said O'Bannon. "I just wanted my face to be the last thing you saw before my friend here blows you into little pieces and tosses the chunks into the woods."

O'Bannon's face was becoming more vivid by the second. My vision was improving.

"I'm sure we can strike a deal," I said.

"No, son. We can't."

Another vehicle, a silver SUV, pulled into the lot and parked next to the sedan.

"Hang on, boss," said the man with the shotgun. "We've got company."

"Get rid of them."

He tucked the shotgun behind him and walked toward the car. The big man and the cell phone still faced me.

A second later, two quick pops echoed through the darkness.

"What was that?" said O'Bannon.

"I'll tell you what it wasn't," I said. "It wasn't a shotgun."

The big man swatted me off the bench with a right hook. Wiping the dirt from my eyes, I watched as a woman in a beige trench coat and red high-heeled shoes approached. I tried to focus to make out more details, but she stood outside of the wash from the overhead lights.

"What's going on?" said O'Bannon.

The big man tossed the phone onto the ground and reached for a revolver inside his pants. Before he cleared it, two shots tore through his chest. He rolled across the end of the park bench and slumped to the dirt next to me.

I picked up the cell phone and held it in front of me. "Looks like someone had other plans," I said. "I'll see you when I get back to Boston, Alfie." I stood up, wiped the prints from the cell phone, and threw it as far as I could into the woods.

The woman in the trench coat tucked her weapon into a holster on her hip. She leaned down in front of me, and for the first time, I recognized her. Special Agent in Charge Valerie Cheatham.

"What are you doing here?" I said.

"I couldn't lose my CI now, could I?"

18

COMING CLEAN

I HAVEN'T BEEN COMPLETELY honest. Porter and Zoe suspected there was a mole inside Sontag's organization, someone who had provided the feds with enough evidence to bring Sontag down. They were right about the mole, but they didn't know it was me. If anyone in Sontag's Clan knew I had aided a federal investigation, they would have cut out my tongue, slit me down the middle, and stapled me to a billboard in Times Square.

I started working with the FBI three years ago when an NYPD cruiser pulled me over on Third Street. Two men who weren't dressed in NYPD uniforms introduced themselves as agents with the FBI and politely asked me to follow them to the cruiser. One of the agents had his hand tucked inside his JCPenney suit jacket, gripping what I assumed was a government-issued weapon.

They escorted me to the cruiser, where I slipped in the back seat. That's where I met Valerie Cheatham, who was sitting, legs crossed, waiting for me. She introduced herself and then didn't say another word until we arrived at the FBI office in Newark, New Jersey.

AT THE FIELD OFFICE, Valerie led me through a cubical farm where several people made an effort to get a glimpse of me. She showed me into a conference room. It was small; six chairs were neatly tucked tight against a white table.

"Have a seat," she said. "I'll be back in a second."

She returned about five minutes later with two men and a folder. I sat down after they did.

"I'll cut right to it, Connor. We know you're working with Joseph Sontag and we want some information from you."

"I wish you would have mentioned this earlier. It would have saved me a trip to New Jersey."

Valerie motioned to the man on my left. His white dress shirt was too tight and he kept running his finger between his Adam's apple and his tie knot.

"You did quite a stint in military intelligence," he said. "Assignments in Germany, Russia, Afghanistan, Syria, Iraq. Part of your military records are locked, so you must have been into some serious shit."

I didn't say anything.

"Quite a few awards here. Must have been pretty good."

He looked at me, waiting for a response, but I kept my mouth shut.

"Then, Mosul happened."

He pulled out another sheet of paper, which I recognized from the seal at the top and the signature at the bottom. The seal belonged to the US Army's Judge Advocate General's Corps. The signature belonged to me. It was a confession.

"Dishonorable discharge," he said, skimming the document. "Two high-value targets... Interrogations... Multiple violations... Articles 128 and 134 of the Uniform Code. Stop me if any of this sounds wrong."

"No, that's all correct," I said.

"How many Iraqis did you interrogate?"

"Too many to count?"

"How many did you torture to death?"

"Just one."

"That something the army frowns upon, is it? Torturing detainees?"

"One day it was legal, and the next it wasn't," I said. "It was an accident."

"So it cost you your career and five years in Leavenworth."

"They made an example out of you," said Valerie.

"Something like that."

The man in the tight shirt continued. "So you leave Kansas and turn up in New York City. Is that when you started working for Sontag?"

I didn't answer.

"We know you're working for him," said Valerie. "I imagine someone with your skill set is a vital member of his organization."

"Lets cut the shit," I said. "Make your ask so I can say no and get on with my day."

Valerie smiled and leaned forward. "We're building a case against Sontag, and you're going to help us."

"No, I'm not."

"You are. You just don't know it yet."

I glanced at all three agents and waited to see who was going to make the pitch.

"You're trying to figure out what leverage we have, right?" said Valerie. "You don't think we'd drag you all the way out here without something concrete?"

They were toying with me.

"You've got nothing on me," I said.

"That's right," said Valerie. "We don't have anything on you. You covered your tracks pretty well. Not surprising for someone with your background. You're careful. Meticulous." Valerie smiled. "I can't say the same about your father."

"Out with it," I said.

Valerie nodded to the agent sitting across from me, who tossed me a folder. It had crimped corners like it had been jammed in a file cabinet door a few times.

"Albert Harding has quite the record," he said.

I opened the folder to find Albert's black and white mug shot staring back at me. "What do you have on him?"

"Mitch Skinner, I assume you know who that is?"

Mitch Skinner was one of my father's longtime friends. He was about the same age as Albert and did odd jobs in the back-woods of Maine to earn a living. He was usually on the right side of wrong, but like my father, he was keen to get into trouble now and then. As I kid, I remember him running a moonshine operation and a numbers racket. None of his schemes ever turned a considerable profit, but they generated enough income that he never had to take a legitimate nine-to-five.

"What about him?" I said.

"He and your father fucked up," said the agent. "I've got both of them for stealing federal property, a game warden's patrol boat."

I knew what he was talking about. The business about the

stolen boat happened years ago. Mitch and my father ran into trouble with some asshole named Ollie something-or-other. Ollie ran a junkyard outside of Meddybemps, Maine and was what you might call the local crime boss. He was more Keystone Cop than Al Capone, but he was still a dangerous man. Last I heard, he was locked up for real estate fraud. But before that, he did time for stealing a game warden's patrol boat. He didn't so much as take the boat, rather the local PD found it on his property. Mitch and my father were the reason it got there.

"That's what you got?" I said. "A stolen boat?"

"It's a federal crime, Connor. He stole it from a game warden. And the value of the property is more than five grand. It's an easy conviction."

"He'll plead out. He's an old man. No judge is going to sentence him to prison. You're full of shit."

"He's got a record," said the man. "Sentencing guidelines dictate he'll do three to five years even if he pleads out. And once he's on the inside, I doubt he lasts long. I hear he has a mouth on him. I'll wager he gets shivved after less than a week inside. That's if he survives the trial. He'll likely keel over from the stress."

"All I need to do is make a call and they'll pick up your father," said Valerie. "He's screwed, Connor. Unless you help me."

I didn't know if they genuinely had enough to put a case together, but I wasn't about to roll the dice. I only gambled when I knew I could win, and I wasn't sure about this one.

My father was an asshole by most measures, but I would never be able to live with myself if they locked him away for the rest of his life and there was something I could have done to prevent it. If I turned on Sontag, he'd eventually find out and they'd make me disappear forever, so I had to walk a fine line.

"I DON'T HAVE the intimate details to put Sontag away," I said. "I'm not a made man. I work for him on a freelance basis. Cleaning things up from time to time. But I think we can help each other."

"Go on," said Valerie.

"I'll give you what I know on Sontag's operation. How it's structured, who does what, and who you need to be looking into. I'll help steer your investigation. I don't wear a wire. I don't testify. I don't collect evidence. My name never goes public. I'll tell you what rocks to look under, but you have to do the digging. I can't implicate him in specific crimes because, on the outside of the organization, I don't have that information. But, I can give you a roadmap to follow to bring Sontag down without getting myself killed in the process."

"That's not enough," said the agent across from me.

"I'm not on the inside and just because you have something on my father doesn't mean I can magically get access to things Sontag doesn't let me see. I'll help you get him, but I'm behind the scenes."

Valerie looked me over.

"I can help you shorten your investigation by years," I said. "And Albert walks. And you keep my name out of the record."

Valerie and the two other agents left the room. Thirty minutes later, they returned and said we had a deal.

I didn't like cooperating with the FBI, but dangling Albert over me left me no choice. I rationalized I wasn't a snitch because I had no other choice. Had it been my own freedom, I honestly don't know if I would have cooperated, but it wasn't my freedom. It was Albert's.

My reluctant partnership with the FBI was also the real reason for my retirement. While working for Sontag was never a long-term career, my deal with Valerie necessitated my exit. The timing and location of my retirement were expertly executed.

It would take the FBI months to build a case strong enough to dismantle Sontag's operation, and I didn't want to be anywhere near him when they made their move. No one would suspect I had anything to do with it if the dominoes toppled years after I left town. I moved to Boston because I didn't want to look like I was running away from something. Beantown was close enough to stay on Sontag's radar, but far enough away not to get hit by the shrapnel when the feds moved in. It also gave me a chance to help my father fight through his diagnosis.

Over a half dozen meetings, I fed Valerie and two other agents everything they needed to understand Sontag's business. His supply lines, his organization structure, his offshore accounts, his expansion plans, where he met with his associates, the two assassinations I knew about, and everything else I had filed away in the Sontag archives in my noggin.

Sontag compartmentalized his business, so no one had all the answers. It was segmented like a US intelligence operation. No one knew what everyone else was doing. They were only aware of their part of the puzzle. My role in the clan necessitated I cross those responsibility boundaries, which gave me a much clearer view of the operation than I should have had as a freelancer. While I didn't have all the puzzle pieces, I did have all the corners and most of the border. With those in place, the feds could fill in the rest.

The entire time I was feeding Uncle Sam intel, I thought about Albert enjoying his freedom, sipping Long Island Iced Teas he'd likely mixed with the wrong ingredients. Focusing on Albert somehow made my cooperation feel less reprehensible.

By the time I finished, Valerie and her team had three walls of a conference room covered with photographs, timelines, mug shots, printouts, Post-it Notes, and red string tying everything together. It wasn't something I was proud of, but this business usually comes down to doing what you have to do, and Valerie Cheatham gave me no alternative.

19

PROFESSIONAL COURTESY

VALERIE EXTENDED A HAND, helped me off the dirt, and sat down on the park bench next to me. "What in the hell are you doing here, Connor?"

"The two people you just killed hauled me out here in their trunk."

"No, not the park. I meant what are you doing in New York?"

"I came looking for the piece of shit who wanted me killed."

"Explain."

"Someone tried to pop me in Boston and I've followed the trail back here."

"Who?"

"Don't know, but I suspect it's someone in the Sontag Clan. You and your boys didn't let it slip I was working for you, did you? Because, you know, that would be bad."

"No. We didn't let it slip. What do you know? Maybe I can help."

"I doubt that. Unless you've picked up any chatter about

someone hiring a Boston mobster to take me out. Although I assume if you had, you would have tipped me off. Professional courtesy and all."

"I haven't heard anything. You think it's related to Sontag's arrest?"

"Yeah, but maybe not my involvement. You know there's a power struggle inside the clan? People jockeying for the top spot?"

"Yeah. We're eyeballing Declan Porter, Nicky Sontag, and Victor Tan."

"Why are you focused on them?"

"Trade secret," she said.

"I'd put my money on Victor Tan."

"Why?"

"Just think he's willing to do what Nicky and Porter aren't."

She stared at me but didn't say anything. It was a common interrogation tactic. If you don't say anything, the other person feels compelled to keep talking. It wasn't going to work on me.

"Maybe you're right," she said finally.

I rubbed the back of my head. "You know where I can find Nicky?"

"What do you want with him?"

"Just want to talk, that's all."

"That why you went to Brick Henry's home?"

"How long have you been tailing me?"

"Long enough to know you were investigating something, just didn't know what."

"So is that a yes or no on Nicky's whereabouts?"

"That's a no."

"If you throw me a bone, I could wrap this up faster and get the hell out of New York before I end up in another trunk."

"Sorry, Connor. I honestly don't know where he is. But I'd like to find out, so if you've got anything, maybe we can help each other."

I slipped my hand in my pocket and rubbed the scrap of paper between my thumb and forefinger. "Sorry. I got as far as Brick's place, but his wife was as helpful as you're being right now."

"What took you to the library?"

"I needed a computer to follow up on some leads. Nothing promising. I'm back at square one with Nicky."

"If you get a location, I'd like to know."

"I bet you would."

"You owe me." She motioned over her shoulder. "I just saved your life. Technically, twice."

"As far as I'm concerned, you're the reason I'm in this mess in the first place, but thanks for the assist anyway."

"How'd you end up with these guys? I don't recognize them."

"Boston mob. Sontag affiliates. Christ, Valerie, I thought you were investigating these guys."

"We're interested in the executives, not the mailroom." She helped me up from the bench, but the pain in my ribs nearly brought me back down.

"You should get that checked out. I can drop you at the ER."

"No thanks. I'll be fine. I could use a ride to my car though. It's in Brooklyn."

"I know where it is."

She helped me to her the SUV. I stepped over the tall, thin corpse with the two bullet holes in him and climbed into Valerie's government-issued vehicle. "What about these two assholes? Don't you have some paperwork to do or something?"

"I'll call NYPD. They'll take care of it. It's better if my name isn't on the report."

I closed my eyes as Valerie dialed her cell phone.

WHEN I WOKE UP, we were pulling into the Bed-Stuy's public library parking lot.

"How long have you been tailing me?" I asked.

"Since the beach house. Followed you to Brick's place, to the library, and then saw your two friends toss you in the trunk."

"You didn't think to pull them over on the highway? I took a beating back there."

"I wanted to see where they took you. I was hoping it was one of Sontag's men."

"Do me a favor and don't wait for so long next time. Thirty seconds later and you would've found me a little less alive than I am now."

"Hopefully there won't be a next time."

"Right." I got out of the SUV and headed toward my Jeep.

"Connor, be careful," she said. "No one is happy you're here."

"I'm starting to get that impression."

Valerie drove away as I got into my Jeep, fired the engine and drove to Hotel Beacon. My head rang like the inside of a church bell at noon. I needed a handful of painkillers and a few hours of sleep.

20

BROOKVILLE, NEW YORK

I WOKE up the next morning convinced I'd been dragged behind a tractor for ten miles. My head hurt worse than yesterday, and I was certain at least two of my ribs were fractured. Whenever I took a breath, it felt like someone was poking me in the side with an ice pick. All I wanted to do was stay in bed and self medicate, but I had to find Nicky.

Rolling out of bed, I stumbled to the bathroom to take a hot shower. That's where the mirror revealed the extent of the Boston boys' handiwork. My torso looked like a piece of blueberry cobbler. I popped six ibuprofen from my ditty bag and hobbled into the shower.

I stood motionless, letting the hot water cascade over me for at least twenty minutes. Then I gingerly toweled off and got dressed. I couldn't bend at the waist thanks to the cracked ribs, and it took at least ten minutes to slip on my jeans while lying on the bed. The socks took another ten. Once I put myself together, I headed to the hotel lobby. My appetite was somewhere between the Hotel Beacon and the Bed-Stuy public library, so I skipped the breakfast buffet.

Fishing my cell phone out of my pocket, I found the nearest rental car counter. I didn't know if Valerie would continue to tail me, but I wanted to visit the Triton Partnership home alone. Hailing a cab outside the hotel was too risky, because if she had a man on me, I'd be easy to spot. Slipping past any surveillance team meant leaving out the back door, near the loading dock. Since no cabs would be stalking that area, I decided to dial a ride-sharing company. I told the driver where to meet me, and ten minutes later I was sitting in the back of a black Honda Accord en route to the rental car company.

I checked for tails the entire three miles, but nothing roused my suspicion. The Accord dropped me off at the car rental place, and after filling out paperwork for fifteen minutes, I had the keys to a new Lincoln Navigator for eighty-two bucks a day.

According to my GPS, the Triton Partnership home was an hour and a half away. I wrote down the route, turned off my phone, and hit the ignition.

When it comes to tails, there's only so much you can do to spot them. If the FBI is following a high-value target, they're going to use multiple vehicles, usually three, to surveil them. The lead car will pass the suspect or turn off, just as another picks up the tail. They use all sorts of tactics to evade being made, and they're really good at it.

I didn't think Valerie had any reason to put a full surveillance team on me. I wasn't a high-value asset, so if she were following me, it would likely only be one car, and that would be easy enough to spot. The ride-sharing company picked me up in an ally, and unless Valerie put an agent in the lobby to watch for me, they wouldn't know I'd even left the hotel. Still, I kept an eye on my rearview mirror and made several U-turns to see if any vehicles stayed on me. I didn't make my way to the Triton Partnership property until I was convinced I was alone.

I ARRIVED IN BROOKVILLE, New York, around eleven. While most villages on Long Island were upscale, Brookville was something to see. Poverty never showed its face in places like this. Everything was clean—the streets, the sidewalks, even the garbage cans on the curb. Everyone on the street wore their Sunday best, even though it was Wednesday. Red-tinged pear trees lined the main street and every home on the main drag could grace a magazine cover.

My GPS led me to Wolver Hollow Road. The homes grew larger the closer I got to the Triton Partnership property. This was the part of the community where the homes had names. I passed a large brick country estate that had a sign on the front gate, *Monday House*, and wondered if the owner had six others.

Beyond that and a few other estates, I arrived at 1729 Wolver Hollow Road. This property, like the others, was surrounded by a solid wall. The wall was green, the same shade as the roof shingles on a set of Lincoln Logs. The thought of climbing that wall in my current condition made me want to vomit all over the concrete paver sidewalk. Luckily, there was a way to walk straight up to the house. A landscaping company was working at a home on the other side of the street. In neighborhoods like this, there was a good chance this landscaping company tended most of the properties.

I drove the Navigator down the road, made a U-turn, and

parked behind one of the landscaping pickup trucks. The crew was working in the yard and never saw me pull up. They also didn't see me lift the hat with the landscaping company logo off the pickup truck's bumper. I slipped the cap on my head and walked back across the street, trying to stand up as tall as possible despite my aching ribs. I tried the gate that was built into the green wall, but it was locked. Next to the handle was an intercom and call button, and on top of the gate was a video camera. I pressed the button and angled my head so the hat's logo pointed toward the camera.

"Yeah?" said a deep voice.

"Hello. I'm Roger Mathers, district manager with Bayside Landscaping. I was hoping I could speak with the owner of the house about an incident with a member of our landscape crew."

"What kind of incident?"

"One of our groundskeepers was involved in a theft a few houses down the street. We're cooperating with the police, and they've asked us to speak with our customers on the block to ensure there weren't any other issues."

"No. We're fine. Thanks."

The dismissive attitude was a good sign. Whoever was on the other side of that intercom didn't want me coming through that gate. A homeowner should have sounded more concerned and would have at least asked for more details.

I buzzed again.

"I said we're good," the voice said.

"Sir, the police gave me a form as part of the investigation. I'm to have homeowners certify our company has spoken with them and confirmed—"

"I'm not interested in your form. Nothing has been stolen from the home. Thank you."

"If I can't get a signature, the Long Island Police Department is required to visit your home in person to ensure there was no theft and confirm a representative from our company spoke with you. It'll just take a moment."

If Nicky Sontag was in that house, I was betting he'd want to keep a low profile and avoid any police officers visiting the property.

The intercom was silent for a few seconds.

"Alright."

The gate unlocked with a buzz. I twisted the knob and walked along the cobblestone pathway leading to the front door. A moment later, I was knocking.

My only goal was to get inside the house. If once inside I found myself chatting it up with some wealthy Long Island family and not Nicky Sontag, I'd make something up about the theft, ask them some general questions, and be on my way. I'd make some excuse about having left the official police form in my truck, tell them I'd go and get it, and then ditch Long Island and start looking for Nicky all over again.

But I didn't need that plan, because I recognized the person who opened the door. Brick Henry stood in the entrance, his shoulders touching each side of the doorjamb. Brick always traveled with Nicky, so him being here meant Nicky was here. Getting past Brick was the hard part.

Brick wasn't the type of person you wanted to fight unless you knew what you were doing, and even if you did know some technical aspects of fighting and had a strategy, a lot of that goes out the window as soon as you get smashed in the face.

Engaging him one-on-one for any length of time was a losing proposition based on his size alone. I also didn't know how many other people were in the house, and the last thing I wanted was to get tangled up with Brick only to find a half dozen other body-guards holding weapons on me. The plan was to put enough distance between us, draw my weapon, and end this as fast as possible. I didn't want to kill anyone, but he didn't know that.

In the doorway, Brick cocked his head to the side. It was apparent he recognized me, but he didn't realize exactly who I was or why I was there. It might have been my two-year absence or the faded landscaping hat. Whatever the reason, I'd caught him off guard. Using the opportunity to my advantage, I lowered my head and dove for his chest. I launched into his sternum like a cannonball, keeping my head straight so I didn't snap my neck in the process. The force propelled him back inside the home and through the walnut banister, where he bounced off the steps.

I kicked the door closed behind me, reached for my weapon, and leveled it at him before he even realized what happened. I steadied my arms and glanced around the room to see if anyone else was rushing in, but didn't see anyone.

Brick stared at me, not sure what was happening. He rubbed the back of his head and tried to stand up on the steps.

"Brick, listen carefully." I spoke slow and clear because I didn't know how hard his head hit the stairs. "Joseph Sontag sent me to find Nicky. He's in a lot of trouble and I need to get him back to the city as quickly as possible. Where is he?"

"I'm right here, Connor."

I turned toward the voice. Nicky Sontag was twenty feet away aiming a 9mm at me. I slowly lowered my weapon. I wanted to set Nicky at ease, but I didn't want to be completely helpless.

"Nicky, your father sent me. I met with him at MCC." I spit the words out as fast as I could because I didn't know how much time I had to convince Nicky not to pull that trigger. "He wants to set up a meeting with Spiro and Napoli and install you as the new head of the organization."

"Bullshit."

Brick reached for the arm rail and pulled himself up to his feet.

"Were you the one who came after me in Alphabet City?" asked Nicky. "You here to finish the job?"

I'd never seen Nicky fire a weapon and had no idea if he was a proficient shot, but at this close range, it wouldn't take much skill to put a hole in me. I had to talk him down.

"Put the gun down and we'll talk it out," I said. "I don't know anything about Alphabet City. I'm here because of your father. I'm here to help you."

Nicky shook his head. "I think you're here to kill me. Who are you working for? Porter? Victor?"

"I'm only working for Joseph."

"How did you find me?"

"I went to the beach house first, then I checked the property records and found this place."

"You alone?"

That's the type of question you ask before you kill someone.

"Look, Nicky, you've got to trust me. Call Messner and he'll sort this all out. Joseph asked me to find you and then arrange a meeting with Spiro and Napoli. Once you're official, their clans will back you and whoever is coming after you from the inside will have to back off."

The 9mm was getting heavy in his hands and his arm was trembling under the weight.

"Think it through, Nicky."

Nicky was quiet. He was processing it. Brick was now back on his feet, teetering between the second and third step.

I didn't like the silence.

"I don't believe you," said Nicky.

"Call Messner!"

"I don't want to talk to Messner. I trust him about as much as I trust you." He turned to Brick. "Kill him."

I raised my weapon again and darted to my left so I had Brick and Nicky in front of me. As far as I knew, there was no one else inside the house. Brick took a step toward me.

"I didn't come here to kill anyone, Nicky. Don't force my hand."

Brick inched toward me, taking another step. He was almost back on the hardwood floor when the first round of bullets came through the front window. The pops came like a Fourth of July fireworks finale. Glass from the windows shattered and blew throughout the living room, curtains bouncing up and down from the gunfire.

I've never been caught in a crossfire before and the feeling is like nothing I've ever experienced. Part of your brain is trying to figure out what's happening, another part is telling you to stay put, and another is yelling to get the hell out of there. Equal parts of your brain pulling you in different directions like some mental game of tug-of-war, only with much higher stakes.

Brick was hit immediately. A shot tore through his left

shoulder, spinning him around and sending him into the staircase for the second time. He took another hit on the steps and then rolled back toward the front door. I was standing in the archway separating the living room and dining room, directly across the room from Nicky. I dove to the ground as glass shattered all around me and crawled through the dining room. I made it to the rear of the dining room, where another archway led back into the living room. I steadied myself in the center of the entrance to take cover from rounds carving up the house. Peering across the living room, I saw Nicky had taken a similar route, maneuvering through what I suspected was the kitchen until he too reached the entrance to the living room on the other side of the house. We stared at each other as shards of glass, drywall, and sofa fabric flew between us.

It was constant fire; just when I thought it was slowing, it picked up again. Round after round smashing into walls, mirrors, photographs, lamps, and the television. Pieces of plaster exploded off the wall, floating in the air like chalk dust.

Brick was crawling toward the sofa in the middle of the living room, leaving a trail of blood behind him. When he made it to the sofa, he reached underneath it and pulled out a black pump-action shotgun that looked to be military grade. He rolled onto his back, lifted his head slightly off the floor and took aim at the still closed front door, the muscles on the sides of his neck straining. The shelling stopped. It seemed like an hour had passed since the first rounds shattered the windows, but it must have been only thirty seconds.

The front door flew off its hinges and two men charged in. Brick fired his shotgun, blowing the first man's leg clear off at the knee and sending the second man to the ground with a hole in his side. He racked the action, ejecting the spent shell into the air and onto the floor behind him.

He turned toward Nicky. "Get out the back," he yelled. "The Buick. Route two." Nicky didn't hesitate. He bolted toward the glass door at the back of the living room, which somehow was still intact. He snapped the deadbolt open and ran out into the back yard. I followed as Brick fired another blast toward the front of the house.

Nicky was charging toward a door in the green wall behind the house.

"Nicky, stop!" I yelled. "They'll be watching the back!"

Nicky wasn't thinking about anything except getting through that door, disregarding whatever might be on the other side. He struggled to turn the deadbolt and unlock the door, which gave me enough time to catch up to him. I raised my .45 as he finally unlocked and opened the door. We went through one after the other.

Brick fired the shotgun again. More rounds of machine gun fire followed his blast.

Two men were waiting on the other side of the fence. They weren't expecting to see us, because neither had a weapon at the ready, probably confident the barrage of gunfire inside the home had done its job.

Upon seeing us, the first man reached for a piece inside his coat pocket. I put two in his gut before he could clear it.

The second fumbled for a shotgun lying on the grass in front of him, but I put two into his chest, dropping him before he secured the weapon. Nicky stopped, and for the first time, he realized I wasn't there to kill him.

We were standing on the street behind the house that ran parallel to the street where I had parked the rental car. Nicky peered down one side of the road and then the other, looking like he was lost. I remembered what Brick had said about "route two." He must have been referencing a preplanned escape route.

I grabbed Nicky by his shoulders and spun him around to face me. "Nicky. Brick said route two. Where is the Buick?"

He thought for a moment. "Two blocks. Follow me."

He crossed the street and I followed him, my .45 still raised. We cut through the side yard of an estate that looked more like a hotel than a home until we reached another road. Nicky turned left and we ran down that street until we arrived at a narrow side road. There, parked on the corner, was a dark-brown Buick Enclave. Nicky reached the car first, knelt, and reached underneath the front driver wheel well. He retrieved a key fob that had been attached underneath the car and tossed it to me.

"Get me out of here."

I took the key, unlocked the car, and we both climbed in. I fired the engine and pulled onto the street, took a sharp right, and headed toward I-495.

We'd driven five miles in silence when I realized I was still holding the .45 in my hand. I slipped it into my coat pocket, adjusted the rearview mirror, and turned to Nicky in the passenger seat.

"The two men at the rear gate," I said. "Did you recognize either of them?"

He stared back at me with a blank expression.

"Did you recognize either of them, Nicky?"

He slumped down in the passenger seat. "I recognized them. They work for Victor Tan."

21

ROAD RAGE

WE'D BEEN on the road for less than ten minutes and had just turned onto I-495 when a black SUV pulled alongside our Buick. I peered over just in time to see the window lower and the barrel of a shotgun emerge from inside the vehicle. I wasn't sure, but it looked like Brick's pump-action model. I grabbed Nicky by the sleeve of his shirt and yanked him down toward the gearshift as I hit the brakes. The shotgun fired, spraying buckshot across the Buick's hood.

Most of the buckshot cut across the front of the car, but I didn't hit the brakes quickly enough to spare the driver's window. Shards of glass exploded into the vehicle, bouncing off the dashboard, Nicky, and me.

I swerved to the right and onto the shoulder. The rumble strip shook the inside of the car as I fought to keep control against the uneven terrain. A panel van passed me on the left, its horn blaring as it blew by. The black SUV had pulled off the other side of the road and was closing the gap in reverse. I wasn't going to let the SUV get parallel and fire off another shot, so I slammed my foot onto the accelerator hard enough to bury it in the floorboard. The Buick surged forward, straddling the right edge of the highway and taking out a mile marker. It would take the driver of the SUV a few seconds to stop, jockey back into gear and pull out into traffic. I used those precious moments to my advantage, quickly overtaking the van and putting about a dozen cars between us.

The SUV was back on the road, and cars were beginning to slow down and give it space, sensing something was happening.

Up ahead, there was an exit for Glen Cove Road, our best chance to ditch the highway. I took the exit and turned right onto Glen Cove without braking, blowing through a red light and nearly clipping a UPS truck. The traffic was more congested here than on the highway, and I weaved in and out of vehicles trying to put as much distance between us and the SUV as possible. I could still see it in my rearview and had to figure out a way to shake the tail before it caught up to us. Up ahead, I saw my chance.

The Greenvale Hospital was ahead on the right. I punched through another red light. The black SUV swerved around the stopped traffic and closed on us. I took a sharp right into the hospital parking garage, drove a hundred feet down the entrance lane, and put the Buick in park.

"Get out of the car," I said, as I opened the driver door.

Nicky followed me and we crouched behind a row of parked cars waiting for the black SUV to pull in. Twenty seconds later it rolled into the garage and stopped twenty feet behind our idling Buick. The man with the shotgun slipped out of the passenger door, crouched down, and approached the vehicle. When he was in range, I stood up from behind the row of cars and fired a shot through his upper chest. He slumped to the cement floor, dropping his weapon. The driver shifted into reverse as I ran out and grabbed the shotgun. I fired two bursts into the SUV. The first shot took out the entire windshield and the second tore through the driver. The SUV continued to roll backward at an awkward angle until it veered into the wall.

I ran to the SUV and checked for anyone else inside. It was empty.

"Come on!" I ran back to the Buick with Nicky behind me. A moment later we were exiting the other side of the garage, retracing our route to I-495.

"The plates on the car, are they traceable to you?"

"No, they're registered to a shell company in Queens. Why?"

"Because it's not going to take long for the police to lift the plates from the garage surveillance cameras. I think we've got enough to deal with."

"We still have to get rid of it."

"Right." I pulled off the road and dialed my cell.

Zoe Armstrong answered on the other end.

"I need two favors," I said.

"What?"

"I'm on Long Island and need to ditch a vehicle. I could use a pick up and transportation to your place. I have to get off the street ASAP, and a cab isn't going to be safe."

"I knew it wouldn't take long for you to screw something up. Why are you coming here?"

"I've got a package I need you to store for twenty-four hours or so. At least until things cool off."

"Where are you on Long Island?"

"I'm sitting in the parking lot of Fresh Meadow Country Club."

She was quiet for a moment.

"Hang tight. I can have someone pick you up in twenty minutes."

"Grab us at the cafe across the street from the country club."

"He'll be there."

"Thanks, I owe you."

"I'll put it on your tally."

"See you soon."

"Connor," she said. "What's the package I'm holding for you?"

"Nicky Sontag."

I WIPED down the inside of the Buick and left it wedged between two maintenance vans at the country club. It would take some time for the local police to get the vehicle description from the garage cameras and then organize a search party. Upscale towns like this one don't have large police forces and aren't staffed to canvas the city. By the time they got their shit in order, we'd be long gone. Nicky said the car was registered to a ghost company, so even if they did find it, which eventually they would, they wouldn't be able to tie it to anyone.

Nicky and I crossed the street, took a seat inside the cafe where we could keep an eye on the parking lot, and ordered coffee. Nicky didn't drink coffee, but he was willing to choke it down to keep up appearances.

I grabbed my cell phone and dialed Messner. It took some convincing to get past Tabitha, his gun-toting secretary, but she finally put me through.

"I'm sure Sontag filled you in on the plan to get Nicky in front of Spiro and Napoli," I said.

"He told me."

"You need to set it up then. For tomorrow."

"You need to find Nicky first," he said. "Good luck with that."

"Nicky is sitting right next to me."

"Bullshit," said Messner.

I held up the phone and Nicky leaned in.

"Hello, asshole," he said.

"How'd you find him?"

"No reason to get into that. Make the call. We need to get this done quick. Tomorrow quick. I'm not sure how long I can keep him underground."

"Alright. I'll make the call."

"Call me back at this number and let me know when and where."

"Fine. Where are you going to put him? I can schedule the sit-down nearby."

"I'll keep that to myself. Do it in the city. I'll be sure he gets there safely." I clicked off the phone and watched a red minivan pull into the handicapped parking spot in front of the window.

"That's our ride," I said, remembering Cricket's vehicle. "Time to go."

CRICKET AND HIS DRIVER, Bob, took us to Harlem and dropped us off behind Hoster Hall. I needed to stash Nicky someplace safe. Victor's men found us at the house in Brookville, and while I was confident they'd lost our scent in the hospital parking garage, I couldn't be sure they wouldn't pick it up again. The longer we were in the city, the more likely Victor Tan could find us. The FBI was also out there, likely looking for me, and I couldn't risk them pulling me and Nicky off the street. My only objective at this point was to keep Nicky safe until tomorrow when I could get him in front of Sontag's two-man commission.

Zoe wasn't happy to see us when we stepped through the back door.

"Please tell me no one knows you're here," she said.

"No one besides you, Cricket, and Bob."

"Come on." She led us downstairs into her furnished apartment.

"How long are we talking about?"

"We're out tomorrow. That's it."

"I don't like it." She turned to Nicky. "You're as volatile as they come right now. Any idea who's looking for you?"

"Victor Tan," said Nicky. "He'll send Eddie Nash. He's the one who took a shot at me."

"That right?" said Zoe.

"You know this Eddie Nash?" I said. "I've never heard of him."

She hesitated for a moment. "Yeah, I know him."

"Bad news?"

"The worst." She walked toward the stairs leading up to the club. "If I were smart, I'd toss the two of you out on your asses and remove myself from the equation."

"Zoe, you're all we've got right now. We'll be out in the morning."

"Victor Tan has eyes all over the city. Assume you've already been compromised, Connor. I'll post a team inside the club, but if Eddie Nash knows you're here, that's not going to be enough."

"No one knows we're here. Unless Cricket—"

"My men are solid. They won't talk."

I waited for Zoe to get upstairs before grilling Nicky.

"Why didn't you tell anyone Victor was the one gunning for you? You could have ended this right away. Why go into hiding?"

"You've been gone a while, Connor. Things change."

"Enlighten me."

He sat on the couch and leaned his head back against the wall. "It's no secret I wasn't the first choice to take over the clan. Everyone was ready to sell me out if it meant I disappeared. There wasn't anyone I could go to."

"What about Porter?"

"You're naive if you think Porter wouldn't slit my throat given the chance. I don't even trust Messner. You've put a lot of faith in him. How do you know he's not sending us into a trap?"

"Messner knows your father wants you in charge. He sure as shit isn't angling for your chair. He'll do the right thing."

"Jesus Christ, Connor."

"Look, I don't trust him either, but he's worked for your father for decades and—"

"That doesn't make him loyal."

"You're going to have to stick your neck out there sooner or later, Nicky. I don't trust anyone in this city, but Messner is all we've got."

"Allegiances change around here every time the wind blows." He stared at me. "Speaking of loyalties, why in the hell are you back here? I don't believe my father pulled you back in just to find me."

"He didn't. Someone tried to kill me. I thought Joseph was behind it, so I came to settle things. You were just a side gig once I got here."

"Why would my father come after you?"

"He didn't. Now I know it wasn't him. It was Victor Tan."

"Why? It doesn't make any sense. What does Victor get by killing you? You're not even in the game."

"Who knows why he came after me. When I get Eddie Nash face-to-face, I'll ask him. Before I blow his head off."

"You think pretty highly of yourself."

"It's too much of a coincidence. Someone comes after you and then me? They have to be connected. I've talked to Porter, Messner, Sontag, and Gretchen. They each gave me a piece of the puzzle, and now you've given me the rest."

"If you've talked to Gretchen, then Victor knows every move you've made."

"What?"

"Gretchen is sleeping with him. Started seeing him after they picked up Joseph. Hell, maybe before they picked him up, I don't know."

I thought back to my conversation with Gretchen in the Palm Court and her invitation to go back to her room. There's a good chance I dodged a literal bullet by walking out of that restaurant when I did.

"When I saw her, she tried to convince me that you were behind the hit on me," I said.

"Now it's starting to make sense." He shook his head.

"How's that?"

"Maybe Victor didn't want you dead. Maybe he just used

you to find me. Maybe he sends someone after you, someone he knows is going to fail. He knows you'd look into things and eventually follow the bread crumbs back here. Gretchen points you in my direction. You track me down, show up on my doorstep just in time for Victor's men to shotgun me in my safe house."

"That seems like a long shot. A lot would have to fall into place for that to happen."

"And yet, that's exactly what happened. Maybe Victor tricks you into finding me, they rub me out, and Victor get his promotion."

Nicky might be onto something, but that was a complicated plan, and complicated plans rarely work. There was too much that could go wrong, and I don't believe Victor could pull all those strings. Or maybe Nicky was right and I just didn't want to admit I'd been played.

"I'll get to the bottom of that later," I said. "Right now, I'm only concerned with getting you in front or Spiro and Napoli."

"I'll make you a deal. If you get me in front of that commission and they sign off on my father's plan to put me on top, then I'll take care of Victor and Eddie for you. I'll even let you watch."

I was thinking of what Nicky's retribution might look like when my phone rang. It was Lyle Messner.

"I set up the meeting," he said. "Tomorrow, ten a.m. The Gramercy Park Hotel. Room 722."

"Seven twenty-two. Got it. We'll be there."

I clicked off the phone and turned to Nicky. "Now we just have to lay low until tomorrow morning."

Nicky nodded and stared at me like he was trying to figure something out. "Why are you helping me?" he asked.

"I told you. Your father asked me to find you."

"I know that, but why are you doing it? You don't owe my father anything. And you hate me. So why do it?"

"I don't hate you, Nicky. I just didn't have any reason to like you."

"What's the difference?"

"Maybe there isn't one. When I first came here, you were on my short list of people I thought might want me dead. I'd planned to find you anyway. It didn't much matter that Joseph asked me to do it too."

He nodded again. "Well, thanks for what you did back there in Brookville. And for what you're doing now."

"You're welcome."

22

WILD NIGHT AT HOSTER HALL

I HAD BEEN asleep for a few hours when I awoke to the sound of screaming and gunfire. Nicky was already watching the video monitors mounted to the basement wall. Still as a statue.

"They're here," he said.

"Who?"

He pointed to the middle screen. "Eddie Nash and his men. They're here for us."

I looked at the screen to see a mob of customers running out the front door and a half dozen men firing toward the back of the club.

"They're here for us," he repeated.

He was babbling something about staying in Brookville as I snatched my .45 from the inside of my jacket and went for the stairs. I took them two at a time and threw my shoulder into the door, knocked it open and stumbled into the rear of the club behind the stage. My body had almost forgotten about the pounding it took at the hands of Brick's brother-in-law and Alfie's men, but the collision with the door phoned in a reminder.

I emerged from behind the stage to find the bartender who had served me the root beer two days earlier firing a submachine gun toward the front of the club. He wasn't used to the weapon and was firing wildly, the recoil knocking him about. Zoe appeared from his side, fired off two shots from her own weapon and ducked behind the bartender, who ejected his spent magazine.

One of Nash's men rose from behind the front of the bar and I fired off six rounds, waiting two seconds between each to give the bartender enough time to reload. I scanned the front of the club but didn't see anyone else. Once the bartender was locked and loaded, Zoe slipped over to me and pushed me back behind the stage.

"You and Nicky have to get out of here," she said.

"Where's the rest of Nash's men?"

"Outside. Regrouping. We don't have a lot of time."

One of the front windows shattered and a flaming bottle smashed against the floor. A wall of flame erupted up to the ceiling and engulfed several nearby tables. A few seconds later, another flaming cocktail exploded inside the club, filling the front section with thick, black smoke and triggering the sprinkler system.

The bartender began firing again and Zoe grabbed my head and tilted my ear toward her mouth.

"Get Nicky. Take the tunnel behind the refrigerator." She was yelling, but I could barely hear her over the machine gun. "Take the white panel van to West Harlem Piers. Look for Virgil." She slammed a set of keys into my hand. "White panel van. West Harlem Piers. Virgil. Go!"

She pushed me toward the trapdoor, raised her weapon and started firing toward the front of the club.

When I reached the bottom of the steps, Nicky was still standing in front of the monitors, which were now completely blurred out thanks to the smoke. I pushed him away from the monitors, knocking him out of his trance.

"Come on, we're out."

I jumped over the kitchen counter and jerked the refrigerator out from the wall. A sharp pain lit up my side causing my jaw to go numb.

There, behind the refrigerator, was an old delivery tunnel, possibly from the days of prohibition. Nicky pushed past me and darted into the tunnel without hesitation. I followed behind, as he used the glow from his cell phone to light our way. A few minutes later, we reached a door at the other end of the tunnel. Opening it, we found ourselves in the back room of a hair salon. I unlocked the salon's back door, which led to a small parking lot. There, sitting next to a station wagon, was a white panel van.

"That's our ride," I said.

I unlocked the doors and we were on our way to West Harlem Piers. It was a little past midnight, and had it not been for our ten a.m. meeting at the Gramercy Park Hotel, I would have jettisoned Zoe's plan and put a few hundred miles between us and Manhattan. Instead, I took the Henry Hudson Parkway to the pier and waited.

A moment later, a security guard ten years past mandatory retirement age rapped a heavy black flashlight on the passenger window. Nicky cracked it.

"You Connor?"

"Who's asking?" I said.

"Virgil."

I nodded.

"Park over there and get out of the van," he said.

"You sure we can trust this guy?" asked Nicky.

"Don't have a lot of options at the moment."

"How do you think Nash found out we were at that club? One of your friend's men must have talked. How do you know this one won't rat us out too?"

"If Zoe wanted us dead, we wouldn't have made it out of that basement. She's solid. I trust her."

"Hope you're right."

I parked the van and we stepped out to find Virgil waving us over to an electric golf cart. He drove us down the pier until we reached a row of five industrial shipping containers. Virgil stopped the cart, shuffled over to one of the containers, unlocked and opened it, and waved us over.

"You've got to be fucking kidding me," said Nicky.

"It'll only be for a few hours," I said. "Until the heat passes."

He shot me a look but didn't respond.

We left the golf cart and approached the shipping container. There were six beds inside.

"Not The Plaza," said Nicky.

"It's made to keep you alive," said Virgil. "Not made for comfort." He held out a weathered hand. "Need your cell phones."

"Why?"

"Zoe said to collect 'em. Figures they're bugged." He waited with his hand out. "You'll get 'em back."

We handed over our phones and stepped inside the container.

"I'll open ya up in the morn'n. Get some sleep. Ain't nothing else to do in there."

"Except suffocate," said Nicky.

"Yeah, I guess that too."

Virgil struggled against the weight of the door, but he finally won out and closed us in. I listened as he slid the vertical metal rod into place and clamped the lock shut.

"How much air you figure we've got in here?"

"Try not to think about it," I said. "Get some sleep. We got a long day tomorrow."

I felt around for the bed and laid down. The inside of the container was so dark I couldn't tell if my eyes were closed or not. I thought about all the ways we could have been compromised. Messner didn't know we were staying at Zoe's place. Nicky was right; someone in Zoe's organization had to give us up. While I trusted Zoe, I couldn't say the same about anyone working for her. Victor Tan and Eddie Nash wanted Nicky dead, and they had the financial resources to buy anyone they wanted.

I hoped Virgil wasn't on that list.

THE CONTAINER DOOR swung open at nine a.m. I was sitting on the bed with my .45 in my hand. Not that I could see to shoot anything, because the bright sun temporarily blinded me as it chased away the darkness inside the container.

When my vision returned, Zoe, Virgil, and a man I'd never seen before stood in front of me.

"I see you're still alive," I said. "Did you get Eddie Nash?"

"No. He torched my place and then disappeared. I've got eyes out for him. I'll get him."

"Sorry about your club."

"We'll settle up on that later," she said.

"How did they find us, Zoe? No one knew we were there."

"I don't know yet, but I'll get to the bottom of it."

"Cricket?"

"Got no reason to believe he's anything but loyal," she said. "Either of you make any cell phone calls from my place?"

Nicky climbed out of the bed next to mine, his hands rubbing his face.

"I didn't call anyone," I said, turning to Nicky. "You?"

"One or two."

"Who'd you call?" I said.

"I called Brick's cell phone. Wanted to see if he made it out of the ambush in Brookville."

"Who else?"

"Victor Tan. Told him I was going to put a bullet through his head."

"Jesus Christ."

"I didn't tell him where I was."

"Maybe he traced your incoming call," said Zoe. "I've got someone looking at both your phones. I'll let you know if we find anything."

"I need a—"

Zoe tossed a cell phone in my lap before I could finish my sentence.

"Make sure I get it back," she said. "Where are you going from here?"

"We've got a meeting to get to."

23

HOTEL ILLNESS

ZOE'S DRIVER dropped us off in front of the Gramercy Park Hotel on the corner of Lexington Avenue and East Twenty-First Street. If Victor was somehow tracking Nicky or me through our cell phones, his signal died when Zoe snatched our phones last night. He'd have no idea we were here, but I wasn't about to get lazy with Nicky. He was still my responsibility until he walked out of that hotel room as the head of the Sontag Clan.

I went through the front doors first, my hand gripping the .45 stashed in my jacket pocket. Nicky was a step behind me, walking close like a person waiting for someone to take a shot at them.

Even though Eddie Nash had been in Zoe's club last night during our brief firefight, I had no idea what he looked like. I asked Nicky to scrutinize everyone in the lobby. He'd recognized Victor Tan's men at the home in Brookville and could do it again. Nicky took his time, checking each face.

Once he was satisfied the lobby was clear, we moved across the black-and-white tile floor, passed the grand staircase and red-carpet waterfall, then reached the elevator bank. I pressed the call button and we waited, my hand still inside my pocket and Nicky still standing close. When the door opened, a man in a suit carrying a newspaper exited and we stepped in. I pressed the button for the seventh floor and we started upward.

The elevator dinged as we passed each floor, finally coming to a rest on seven. The door opened and I peered out. The floor was empty except for a maid's cart parked between guest rooms.

We stepped out into the hallway. A brass placard directed us to room 722. We moved down the hallway side by side. I spent most of the time looking behind me. We reached 722, but before knocking, I pressed my ear to the door. I could hear faint talking. Idle chatter, but nothing discernible.

I'm not an easy person to rattle. The US Army trained me how to stay calm in most situations, how to keep the blood pressure down, and the shakes away. When that shit creeps in, you start thinking funny, and that's when bad things happen. I'd been able to keep it together since arriving back in New York, but for some reason, standing in front of that solid black door made something click inside me. Doubt crept in, and I had the urge to run for the first time in a long while. I pushed it back down inside from wherever it came from and knocked on the door.

We waited. I glanced at Nicky, who appeared more relaxed than I'd seen him in the last twenty-four hours.

There were footsteps on the other side of the door. My muscles tightened and the .45 was heavier in my hand. It felt like I was carrying a boat anchor inside my jacket pocket.

The knob turned and the door opened slowly. A bald man

wearing a black polo shirt underneath a light gray sport coat ushered us in.

In front of us were two chairs: one brown leather and the other red velvet. Between the chairs was a three-wheeled liquor cart with mirrored shelves. It was stocked with top-shelf bottles and crystal glasses. My hand was still in my pocket, and I waited for the man in the gray sport coat to pat me down, but he didn't.

"Mr. Spiro?" he said, looking toward the bedroom.

Alfred Spiro, boss of the Spiro Clan, walked out of the room. He looked to be pushing eighty. He was thin and frail, but looked the part in his three-piece, charcoal-gray suit with a red handkerchief sticking out of his breast pocket. He shook Nicky's hand and took a seat on the leather chair. A moment later, Armand Napoli walked out of another bedroom. He was younger than Spiro by a good twenty years. He sported a crew cut and a thin neck. He nodded at me, shook Nicky's hand, and sat next to Spiro.

I'd never witnessed a mob initiation before, but I assumed it wasn't like the movies where someone slices their palm open and bleeds on a table in front of everyone before taking an oath of loyalty. That was for show. This was more transactional, an official passing of the torch from Joseph Sontag to his son. After this moment, the Spiro and Napoli clans would recognize Nicky as the sole leader of the Sontag Clan. And that meant everyone else in the Sontag organization would have to accept him too. Anyone trying to replace him with an unsanctioned hit would face the swift and violent fury of Spiro and Napoli. That's how they kept the peace—cooperation. No one wanted a war, because those are bloody and unprofitable.

After this meeting, Nicky would likely appoint an advisor,

who would put the word out that Nicky was in charge. That proclamation would force Victor Tan, Eddie Nash, and anyone loyal to them to leave the city if they wanted to keep breathing. Nicky would go after them of course with the full resources of the Sontag organization. If they pulled in someone like Zoe and her Whisper Network, which they probably would, they'd remove Victor and Eddie from the gene pool within a week. Two weeks tops.

Spiro and Napoli motioned for Nicky to sit down. He did so, sitting with his legs open wide and his palms on his knees.

"Shall we begin?" said Spiro.

With that, two men stepped out of the suite's third bedroom. I recognized one of them immediately: Victor Tan. I assumed the other man, a younger man in jeans and a zip-up black sweater, was Eddie Nash, Victor's triggerman. Before I realized what was happening, Nash raised a pistol from his side and fired three rounds into Nicky. Nicky and the chair he was sitting in tumbled to the ground. Nash raised the gun toward me and fired, but I dove through the open bedroom door on my right, pulling my .45 as I landed next to the bed. I fired two shots blindly into the suite's main room and the men scattered. Kicking the door closed, I locked it and jumped behind the bed. Someone tried the handle and I sent two more slugs through the door, about a foot above the crystal knob.

I didn't have much time. They'd be organizing on the other side. If I stayed in here, this was only going to end one way. That door would come down, probably blown off its hinges with a shotgun they had stashed in one of the other bedrooms. A second burst from the same shotgun would end me. I didn't plan on bleeding to death in a suite in the Gramercy Park Hotel, but that meant moving quickly. I fired two more shots through the door and rushed to open the bedroom window. Most hotels seal their windows shut to save on air conditioning costs. Lucky for me, the Gramercy didn't care about their energy bills. If they had, I'd be looking for a way to smash through the window, but instead, I was looking seven stories down at a paved alley. It was narrow, and the area below was more suited for foot traffic than vehicle traffic. On the other side of the alley stood a luxury apartment building. I gauged the gap between the two buildings to be twelve to sixteen feet, which meant I was close enough to jump the gap and hit one of the balconies on the other side. I'm six-foot-one, so the length of my body alone would get me almost halfway across the alley. Factor in a solid boost off the concrete window ledge and I'd clear the distance. Hitting one of the balcony railings below was going to hurt like a bitch, but I'd take that pain over whatever awaited me if I stayed in this hotel room.

The bedroom door swung open and someone fired a barrage of shots inside the bedroom. The first round slammed into the metal suitcase sitting on the plush bed. The next two found their way into the wall, and the fourth and fifth rounds shattered the window I'd just opened.

I returned fire from the floor behind the bed to push them back into the main room. My shots gave me a few seconds and I didn't take them for granted. I slipped out the window onto the narrow ledge and grabbing the bottom of the window frame for balance, I crouched low, squatting, feeling the tension building in my legs. I had to get the angle right. Jump too soon and I'd never clear the distance. Jump too late and my body would be too flat to grab the balcony and stick the landing. After doing a few seconds of mental geometry, I released the window frame, let myself fall forward until I was satisfied

I had the right angle, and sprang from the ledge, pushing off with the balls of my feet. My brain didn't have time to process what I had done before gravity and momentum slammed me into the white, modern steel balcony railing attached to the building behind the hotel. I nearly lost my weapon upon impact but somehow was able to hang onto it. Pulling myself over the rail, I tumbled onto the floor, crashing into a ceramic flower pot.

As a bullet ricocheted off the balcony floor cracking another flower pot, I dragged myself behind a ten-foot tall artificial palm tree. I raised my .45 to return fire, but my right hand was shaking too violently to aim. I must have crushed it against the balcony railing when I jumped, I just hadn't noticed it.

Switching hands, I took aim and squeezed the trigger. The weapon clicked. My .45 held seven rounds in the magazine and one in the chamber. I was spent.

One of Victor's men was climbing out the window, steadying himself to make the same jump to the balcony. I plunged my shaking hand inside my jacket and yanked a spare magazine out. I ejected the empty magazine, slammed the new one into the weapon, chambered the round, and fired. The slug found whoever was climbing out of the hotel window. He reached for the windowsill but lost his grip. Tumbling out the window, he fell seven stories to the street below.

Nash peered out the window and fired. The shot was true, and the slug exploded into my right thigh. There wasn't much pain, thanks to the adrenaline surge, and had it not been for the small splatter that sprayed from my thigh, I'm not sure I would have even realized I'd been hit.

The bullet struck me in the middle of my thigh near the

edge of my leg. It was a clean shot, straight through, several inches from my femoral artery. That shot wasn't a death sentence, but staying on this balcony was. Victor would have sent someone over to the apartment complex, and I couldn't risk getting caught in this choke point.

Nash was aiming again when I returned fire. I'm not a solid shot with my left hand, but this one landed close, smashing into a brick just to the left of Nash's head. He reeled backward and disappeared into the bedroom.

Turning to the sliding glass door behind me, I drove my boot heel into it with all the strength I had left. My leg throbbed with each blow. It took five kicks to shatter the door. I kept kicking until I'd opened up a hole large enough to crawl inside the apartment. Luckily, no one was home.

Safely inside the apartment, I checked my thigh. Given the location of the gunshot, I wasn't bleeding enough to worry about it, but I still had to stop whatever was spilling out of my leg. On my way to the apartment's front door, I snatched a cloth placemat from the kitchen table, folded it diagonally, and tied it around the upper part of my thigh a few inches above the wound. The tourniquet made it difficult to walk, but I kept moving.

Opening the apartment door, I stepped into the hallway and toward the elevator. I knew Victor was one man down but had no idea how many other men he had. If he knew what he was doing, he would have sent one man up to the sixth floor—I was one level below the bedroom of the Gramercy Park Hotel. He would have stashed another man or two in the apartment complex lobby to intercept me coming down the stairs or elevator. But only if he had the men.

The last thing I needed was to get into a shoot-out in a

narrow stairwell or the hotel lobby, so I had to find another way out.

My solution came via the screeching sound of an electric drill. I followed the sound and turned the corner to another hallway. There, near the end of the hall, was a maintenance worker installing a wall sconce. He likely came up a maintenance elevator. Luxury apartments like this one don't want the maintenance staff mingling with the tenants, so they send them up separate elevators, which would require a passkey to access. The maintenance worker was my hall pass. Any maintenance elevator should also go to the basement, which isn't accessible via the guest elevators.

I stashed the .45 back inside my jacket and limped toward him. He saw me coming, stopped his installation, and jumped off his ladder.

"You okay, pal?"

According to the embroidered patch on his blue coveralls, his name was Mike.

"Mike, I need to get on the maintenance elevator."

"From the looks of it, ya need to get to a doctor."

"Look, there's some bad people coming up the main elevator. When they get here, they're going to gun us both down. The maintenance elevator is our only way out."

"What are you talking about?"

"We need to go!"

"I'm gonna call the cops." He reached into his tool belt.

"I am the cops. This is an undercover sting gone seriously wrong and we have to get out of here. Now!" I raised my bloody hands from my leg.

His eyes widened at the sight of my crimson palms, and luckily, he didn't question my credentials.

"Christ. Okay, let's go."

He collapsed his folding ladder, tucked the drill under his arm, and hustled down the hallway. I struggled to keep up. We turned another corner and came to the maintenance elevator at the end of the hall. He pulled an ID attached to a zip line on his belt and held it in front of the sensor. The elevator motor whirred and I looked over my shoulder, waiting for Nash's men. About thirty seconds later the elevator opened without a ding and I followed him on.

"Lobby?"

"Basement," I said. "Lobby isn't safe."

He pulled a walkie-talkie from his tool belt. "At least let me call security."

I swatted his walkie-talkie away. "Calling them will make things worse. The people looking for me will leave once they see I'm gone. Calling security will just lead to a shoot-out. Your residents will be safer if you don't call."

He thought for a moment and then slipped the walkie-talkie back into his tool belt.

The elevator jolted to a stop and the door opened into the basement.

"I need a back way out," I said.

"Yeah, okay. Follow me."

He ditched the ladder and drill and guided me through the basement. I stopped when we came to a storage shelf packed with painting supplies. I swiped several clean rags from a box on the lower shelf and pressed them against my leg. The placemat tourniquet had slowed the bleeding, but I was still a mess.

When I was finished mopping up, I followed Mike to a pair of brown metal doors at the back of the basement. He turned the deadbolt and pushed them open. The sun warmed my face as I glanced around to get my bearings. I was standing in a loading dock area. About fifty feet away from the door were four industrial garbage bins with wide, flip-up lids.

"Thanks the for help, Mike."

"Yeah. You sure I can't call—"

"One more question. Do the garbage trucks come today?"

"No. Tomorrow."

I nodded. "The NYPD thanks you, Mike. Now head back inside."

He closed the doors as I limped to the garbage cans and wedged myself between the large metal bins and a retaining wall. I tightened the tourniquet on my leg, pressed a paint rag against the wound, and dialed the spare cell phone Zoe gave me.

She answered three rings later.

"What do you need now? I'm kind of busy mopping up your mess at my club."

"Nicky's dead."

"How?"

"The sit-down was an ambush. Spiro and Napoli were there, but so were Victor Tan and Eddie Nash."

"Fuck."

"They shot Nicky right in front me."

"I'm sorry, Connor. How did they know you were coming?"

"I don't know."

"Maybe I do," said Zoe. "There was a bug on the phone."

"Nicky said he called someone from your club—"

"Not Nicky's phone. Yours."

"What? That's not possible."

"Well, I've got a smashed chip in my garbage can that says

otherwise. According to Cricket, it was pretty sophisticated. It could track you and let someone access your microphone. I'd consider any conversations you've had compromised. Any idea who did it?"

Whoever planted the device inside my phone would have needed to open it. The only time it was out of my sight was in Messner's office, when his secretary took it along with my weapon. And it was on her desk, not in the drawer with my .45, when I took it back.

"I think I have an idea," I said.

"Then you might want to plug that hole."

I glanced down at my leg. "Speaking of holes, I need access to a doctor."

"Then go to a clinic. I don't run a medical practice."

"If I go to a clinic, they'll want to know about the bullet hole in my leg. And they'll inform the police. I'd like that not to happen."

"You've been shot?"

"It's not bad, but it'll get there if I don't get some help."

She thought for a moment. "Where are you?"

"Behind the dumpsters behind the Gramercy Park Hotel."

"That's a fitting place for you. How serious is it? Can you wait twenty minutes or are you gonna bleed out?"

"I can wait."

"Alright. It'll take some time. Keep out of sight. Doc Dresden. Look for an HVAC repair van."

"Got it. Thank you."

"You owe me for this one, Connor."

"Put it on my tab."

"You're overdrawn."

. . .

THE VAN PULLED up in front of the dumpster. The driver tapped the horn twice. I stood up and slipped out from behind the garbage bin and limped to the vehicle. The driver rolled down the passenger window.

"Name?"

"Connor."

He motioned me in.

"What day is it?" asked the driver.

"Thursday. Why?"

"Want to see if you're still lucid. Buckle up. It'll be a few minutes."

Fifteen minutes later, we pulled into the Liberty Harbor RV Park right across the basin from Liberty State Park. Out the window, beyond the boats docked at the adjacent marina, I could see Ellis Island and the Statue of Liberty.

The driver, who never introduced himself, helped me out of the van and into a gleaming black and gold RV. The walls of the RV were lined with all kinds of medical equipment, some I recognized and others I didn't. I had conjured up an image of a back-alley doctor with dull and rusted surgical tools operating out of some abandoned hellhole, but this RV was pristine, smelled like pine needles, and had better equipment than the VA Hospital in Boston.

Dr. Dresden, a young man in a surgical mask, introduced himself and helped me onto a metal exam table at the back of the RV where the bed would usually have been. It was sterile and cold.

"It's clean through," I said.

He gave me an injection and things got cloudy. Dr. Dresden was talking to me, but I couldn't make out what he was saying. His slurred words turned to mumbles and then silence.

I woke up on a sofa behind the driver's seat, my jeans on the floor in front of me. My right thigh was wrapped in what looked like cellophane, like some dinner leftover. I could see the wound through the clear dressing; there were no stitches. I grabbed my jeans from the floor and slowly slipped them on.

The doctor was sanitizing the exam table in the back. "Are you a betting man, Connor?"

"Not really, why?"

"Because I'd guess you've used all your luck for a while. As far as gunshots go, they don't get any better than that. No significant tissue damage, no arterial hemorrhage, and minimal blood loss. Your systolic blood pressure is a little low, but the only thing I'd be worried about is infection given the time the wound was exposed."

He approached and tossed a bottle into my lap.

"Here's a broad-spectrum antibiotic. Take two every four hours for the next three days. If the wound starts to look like something you've left in the back of your refrigerator or if you experience any paralysis, get yourself to a hospital. I don't see repeats."

He helped me off the sofa and I wobbled a bit.

"I gave you an injection for the pain."

"How long will that last?"

"Hard to say. It's different for everyone. Could be a few days."

"What about the dressing?"

"You can remove it after ten days. Otherwise, don't touch it."

"Thanks for the help.

"You're welcome."

I stepped out of the RV as the same van that dropped me off earlier pulled up and squealed to a stop. The driver ran to the back of the van and opened the rear doors. Dr. Dresden jumped out of the RV and looked at the bloody man in the back.

"Want me to help you get him on board?" I asked.

"No need," said Dr. Dresden. "He's dead."

The driver slammed the doors closed and walked back to the cab.

"You going back to the city?" I asked.

"Yeah, why?"

"I could use a ride."

FORTY MINUTES later the driver dropped me off at the Hotel Beacon. I had to assume Victor knew I was staying here, so I slipped in through the back alley in case his men were watching the front door. I wasn't going to stick around, but my next stop was a return visit to see Declan Porter, and I wasn't going to do that before reloading.

24

HEADSPACE

DECLAN PORTER HAD LIED to me. There was no way Victor Tan was making a play for Sontag's throne without Porter knowing something about it. I was going to get to the bottom of it, and then I was going to kill Victor and Nash. It was the only way to keep them from coming after me. The question was how. Killing Victor twenty-four hours ago was one thing, but now he was the official head of a criminal organization, at least according to Spiro and Napoli, and that meant he was protected. Any action against him would be met with swift and certain retribution. Getting close enough to put a bullet in him was one thing, but doing it in a way that didn't sign my own death warrant was something else entirely.

Back at my hotel, I changed out of my bloody clothes and then ducked into the parking garage, where I reloaded my .45 and spare magazine with the ammo from my Jeep's glovebox. I also dropped an extra magazine in my pocket, just in case. I wasn't planning on being in another shoot-out, but I wanted to be better prepared should one arise.

Up ahead in the parking garage, a car flashed its lights at

me. It was a white BMW, not one I'd seen before. It flashed again, and I flashed back. I dragged the slide on my .45 back, loading a round into the chamber as the car rolled forward.

The BMW stopped in front of me and Lyle Messner got out and walked to my driver window.

"I heard about Nicky," he said.

I grabbed his light-blue necktie, wrapped it around my fist and pulled his head down until his chin rested on the business end of the .45.

"You set us up."

"No, I didn't."

"We walked into an ambush. How else did Victor Tan know we were going to be there? Unless you told him."

"I didn't tell him. He must have cut a deal with Spiro and Napoli. They were all in it together. Spiro called me after it was done and said they are recognizing Victor as the new head of the organization and that I was to alert the rest of the clan."

"Bullshit. You tapped my phone. You told Victor that Nicky and I were at Hoster Hall, and when we survived the ambush, you made sure he wouldn't survive the sit-down."

"That's not what happened."

I pushed the .45 into the soft part of his jaw. "You didn't tap my phone?"

"Yes, I did, but not to set you up. I didn't know why you were back in New York, but I knew it wasn't good. I had Tabitha do it as a precaution. It had nothing to do with Nicky."

"Why should I trust you?"

"Connor, I tapped your phone when you first came to my office asking to see Sontag. Long before you had anything to do with Nicky."

Messner was right about that. Tabitha tapped my phone

before Sontag asked me to find Nicky, before I knew anything about the revolution in Sontag's organization.

I loosened my grip on his tie. I wasn't convinced Messner was innocent in all this, but I also wasn't confident he was behind Nicky's assassination.

"Why are you here?" I asked.

"It's Joseph. He wants to see us."

"About Nicky?"

"That's right."

"He already knows?"

"I called him after I got the call from Spiro. I told him what they told me, that they decided to back another horse. It goes without saying that Sontag's not happy with the arrangement, but now he knows Victor was behind everything."

"What does that have to do with me?"

"I suspect he's going to ask you to kill Victor."

"I was planning on doing that anyway. Does he have any idea how to do it so I don't go down with the ship? Sontag's protected by a few feet of concrete. I'm not."

"Only one way to find out. Ask him."

I'll be honest, the idea of sitting across the table from Joseph Sontag and owning the fact I couldn't keep his son alive was concerning, to say the least. I'd done everything I could to keep Nicky alive until we made that meeting, but I didn't know if I could convince Sontag of that.

Still, I was in a mess with Victor and Nash, and if anyone could find a way out of my shithole situation, it was Sontag. He was the type of person who did his best thinking when his back was to a wall, and that's precisely where his back was now. Against a wall. Right next to mine. As much as I didn't want to be in the same room with him, he might be my only way out of this.

"Alright. Get in." I unlocked the passenger door.

"How about I drive?"

"No way. Nash is still out there looking for me. If he tries to take me out on the highway, I want to be the one behind the wheel."

Messner's eyes widened, as if he hadn't thought of that scenario. "Fine." He locked up his car and climbed into the Jeep. A minute later, we were on the FDR en route to MCC.

IT TOOK a half hour to get there. I stashed my weapon under the driver's seat and looked over at Messner. He wore gray slacks, a black mock turtleneck and a camel topcoat, probably cashmere. I wore a pair of light-blue jeans, a gray sweatshirt and my green military jacket.

"They going to let me in?" I said. "In these clothes, I don't look like I belong here."

"Would you rather go back to the hotel and change into that ill-fitting suit? It's not much better." He smiled. "They'll let anyone in as long as they're with me."

A few minutes later, we were in the lobby presenting our credentials to the woman behind the bulletproof glass. She told us Sontag was waiting in conference room two. We walked through the security door, through the metal detector and into the corridor where a guard led us to the conference room.

Unlike my last meeting with Sontag, he was already in the conference room, but this time he wasn't shackled to the chair. Instead, his arms were crossed in front of him and his seat was tilted back on two legs, leaning against the white wall.

Nothing about this was right.

"Sit down," said Sontag.

The guard closed the door behind us.

I took a seat directly across from him. Messner sat at the end of the table to Sontag's right.

"What happened?"

Messner turned to me, both men waiting for my explanation.

"I located Nicky at the house on Long Island. Victor Tan's men followed me there. I'd switched cars to avoid a tail, but they still found me. It's possible they might have tapped my cell." It took a lot not to mention Messner. "They ambushed us in Brookville. Nicky and I escaped. We made it back to the city, where Zoe Armstrong put us up. Victor found us there and sent a hit squad. They torched Zoe's place, but I was able to get Nicky out of that too. We went off the grid until the next morning. Messner had set up the sit-down and we arrived at the Gramercy Park Hotel as directed. Victor Tan was waiting for us in the hotel room. They shot Nicky in front of me."

"How did you get out in one piece?"

Sontag was pressing me. He had multiple scenarios running through his head, and in one of those scenarios, I led Nicky to the slaughter.

"I didn't. There's a bullet hole in my leg thanks to Eddie Nash."

"You weren't limping when you walked in here."

"Painkillers haven't worn off yet. I suspect they will in the next twenty-four hours. I'll drop my pants if you want proof."

"Not necessary," said Sontag, turning to Messner. "And you set up the meeting?"

"That's right, just like you asked."

"Did Victor approach you before any of this went down?"

"No. I assume he had already aligned himself with Spiro and Napoli. Once I set up the sit-down with them, they probably tipped him off."

Sontag nodded. Then he closed his eyes and leaned his head against the wall. A good thirty seconds passed without a word. Messner and I turned to each other, looking for some sign of what to do next.

I was about to speak when the front two legs of Sontag's metal chair slammed into the tile floor. He uncrossed his arms.

"There's something else we need to discuss." He stood up and paced the room. "Ever since they picked me up, I've been convinced someone in my organization was working with the feds to build a case against me. Someone was feeding them intel on my operation. Someone they might even try to put on the witness stand. A key witness. Someone to put me away for a long haul."

I had covered my tracks as far as my cooperation with the FBI went, but my brain was scrambling to figure out what Sontag might know. He was pacing quicker now, and every time he took a step the table vibrated.

"I racked my brain to figure out who would be so stupid," Sontag continued. "Who would betray me like that? Who had something to gain for cooperating with the police? And now I know."

Messner and I looked at each other again.

Why wasn't Sontag shackled? And why wasn't there a guard in the hallway when we entered the conference room like before? I looked up. The video camera in the corner of the room was unplugged.

I had wondered the first time I met with Sontag in MCC

how much influence he had on the inside. Now I had my answer. I'd walked into a trap for the second time today. Sontag had choreographed this entire meeting. The guard at the metal detector was likely gone, perhaps on a stroll to get a cup of coffee. The woman in the bulletproof booth was too isolated to hear anything. The video cameras were off, and I'd wager the rest of the nearby conference rooms were empty. It was just Sontag, Messner and me. Messner was the first to speak.

"What are you talking about?"

"One of our friends in the NYPD came across some information. The name of one of the federal agents on the task force investigating me. Porter and his men picked him up. Took him to Brooklyn where they tortured him with a pressure washer. Porter said they peeled a lot of skin off before they got a name, but they got one."

He stopped next to Messner, leaned across the table and stared straight through me.

"You want to wager a guess on who it is, Connor?"

This is how it happens. This is where Sontag kills me.

"I don't know anything about it, Joseph. I'd never betray you like that. Why would the feds come to me anyway? I couldn't give them anything close to what they'd need to build a case against you."

Sontag stood back up and walked to his chair. My heart started beating again at the thought of him sitting back down and talking this out. Maybe I could reason with him, tell him about my father. Maybe he'd understand since he was a father himself. But he didn't sit down. He picked up the chair, whirled around and crushed it into the back of Messner's head. He struck him so hard, that Messner's head smashed against the table and then ricocheted up again, blood pouring from his nose. He mumbled something and then Sontag slammed the chair into his head again. And then again, and again. When he was done, blood covered half the table and Messner's head was split open, fragments of bone and brain coating the chair still in Sontag's hand.

Sontag flung the bent chair against the wall. He stared at me and I stared back, struggling to process what just happened. Sontag knew something I didn't, and since I was still alive, I figured whatever that was didn't include my involvement with the FBI's investigation.

I raised my elbows off the table to avoid the blood that crept closer to me.

"Messner was working with the FBI," said Sontag.

"Why would he do that?" I asked. Was Messner working with the feds too? Maybe they brought him in independently of me. It's likely they had multiple informants to get a full view of Sontag's operation.

"Who knows," he said. "Maybe they had some leverage on him. It doesn't matter now. They've got what they got, and he's not going to give them anything else."

I looked back at the unplugged camera on the wall. How was he able to set this up? Why weren't an army of guards smashing through the conference room door?

"So, about Nicky," said Sontag, changing subjects like there wasn't a dead attorney with a shattered skull splayed out in front of us.

"I did everything I could, Joseph—"

"I know you did. And I don't hold you responsible for his death. But now I need you to do something else for me. Victor Tan orchestrated a coup. You're going to find him and kill him.

I doubt I'm asking you to do anything you weren't already going to do."

He was right about that.

"You know where I can find him?"

"No clue. Porter probably knows. Given his history with the organization, I don't think Victor can cut him out. Not yet, anyway."

"Right." I wiped Messner's splatter off my face.

"But be careful, Connor. There's a chance Porter's been wrapped up in this for a while. Go in there assuming he's going to kill you. Or at least sell you out. Or talk to Gretchen." He tapped his fingers on the table. "I assume you know about Victor and Gretchen."

"I knew about them, but I didn't know you knew."

"I know everyone she's been with, Connor."

I swallowed hard as Messner's body slid out of the chair onto the floor.

"Once I kill Victor, the entire New York criminal under-world is going to come for me. How are you going to stop that blowback?"

"Cash," he said. "I'll buy your freedom. Don't worry about it."

"No offense, but it's hard not to worry about it."

"Money makes this thing go round, Connor. And I've got a ton of it. You kill Victor Tan, and you'll walk away a free man. I promise you that."

That didn't do much to make me feel any better, but given what Sontag was able to arrange in this conference room, I didn't doubt there were still strings he could pull. I stood up and went for the conference room door.

"And Connor," said Sontag. "Enjoy your vengeance."

I turned the doorknob and stepped into the hallway, unsure what I'd find there. It was empty. No guard. No nothing. I turned the corner, passed the unmanned metal detector, the empty lobby, and walked out the front door.

Any hesitation I had that Sontag had lost his mojo on the inside was gone. He still had enough juice to buy off an entire shift of Bureau of Prison employees. I no longer doubted his ability to buy my freedom after I killed Victor.

But first I had to find him.

25

THE PRODIGAL SON

SONTAG WAS right about the payoff money. He might be able to finance my freedom after I put Victor down, but that wasn't my only concern. There were three crime families in New York, and within the next few days I'd be a wanted man with all three of them. Sontag could likely protect me from any blowback from Victor's death, but Spiro and Napoli would still be on my tail for witnessing Nicky's assassination. I was a loose end and like Sontag said, nothing ties up loose ends like cold hard cash. I knew Spiro and Napoli could be bought because Victor had done just that. He financed the hit on Nicky that put him in the position to take over Sontag's organization. I planned on buying my way out of their crosshairs, but that was going to take the kind of money I didn't have.

I hoped Zoe would float me a loan to get out from under Spiro and Napoli, but her financial help always came with strings, and I had to be careful of what I agreed to. I was a mile away from Hoster Hall when an NYPD cruiser pulled behind me and flashed its lights. I pulled over near Lenox Hill Hospital. The uniformed officer told me to get out of the car and walked me to his cruiser. Valerie Cheatham was in the back seat.

"I'm beginning to think you're using the NYPD as your personal taxi service."

"Cut the shit," she said. "We need to talk." She picked up a folder from the seat between us. "Does the name Alex Werner mean anything to you, Connor?"

"No, why?"

She opened the folder and tossed a glossy photo in my lap. The man in the photo was dead and had been carved up pretty badly.

"That image jog your memory?"

"I don't know who this is."

"This is one of my agents. What's left of him. NYPD pulled him out of a Brooklyn storm drain yesterday. He's on my Sontag Taskforce."

This must be the agent Porter tortured to get the information that Messner was cooperating with the feds. I decided to keep that tidbit in my pocket for now and see where Valerie was going.

"I don't know anything about this," I said.

"Someone in Sontag's organization tortured and killed a federal agent. That doesn't go unpunished. I had to talk to his wife yesterday. I had to tell her I was sorry about what happened to him, and I promised to do everything in my power to find out who was responsible. And that's what I'm going to do. And you're going to help me."

"I came back to New York to find out who wanted me dead, not thin out your task force."

"I don't think you had anything to do with it. It's not your MO. But you are going to help me figure out who did this."

"How's that?"

"You're going to talk to Sontag's men. Find out what they know. And you're going to wire up."

Valerie was running the same play she ran two years ago when she pressured me to get information on Sontag's operation, but this time was different. When I was feeding her intel on Sontag, I could do it my way, take my time and move in a way that didn't shine a spotlight on me. I could tell by her twitching fingers that she wanted to take down whoever was behind her agent's death quickly, and quick usually meant poorly planned, which leads to mistakes and dead informants.

"No way," I said. "I go poking around and it won't take long for them to figure out what I'm up to. And by the looks of that photo, Sontag's men can do worse to me than you can."

"Then I'll just haul you in for it."

"I didn't have anything to do with this."

"I know, but Sontag's people don't. Maybe I haul you in, hold you for a few hours and tell the media we've got a suspect in agent Werner's death."

"That's bullshit."

"Who cares? Sontag's men will be stepping over each other to put you down so you don't talk."

"I don't know anything."

"Don't care. You get me the information I need, or I take you in."

Just like before, Valerie had the leverage she needed to move my hand.

"Alright. I'll see what I can do, but you have to let me do it my way."

She reached into her pocket and handed me a USB thumb drive.

"What's this?"

"It's a transmitter. There's a switch on the bottom. Activate it and it'll transmit your conversation to a recorded line. These things are ubiquitous. Everybody's got one. No one will think twice if they find it on you."

I slipped it in my pocket.

"I want evidence on anyone and everyone involved in agent Werner's death."

"I get this for you and you never show up in my rearview again."

"I can live with that."

Valerie nodded and the officer opened the rear door. I got out but stuck my head back in.

"Now I've got a question for you," I said.

"What's that?"

"Were you working with Lyle Messner? Was he cooperating with your investigation into Sontag?"

"The lawyer? No way. Attorneys are off limits. Why?"

"Sontag was under the impression that Messner was working for you."

"Then I'd hate to be him right now."

"Me too."

I closed the door and the NYPD cruiser sped off before I reached my car.

My to-do list was growing longer, and I was running out of time. I could get Valerie her evidence, but that was going to have to take a back seat to Victor. The longer I stayed in New York the more likely Victor was going to find me. But I like breathing, and I wasn't going to let that happen. I had to kill Victor before he killed me.

I had a small window I could use to my advantage. Nicky's

body wasn't even cold yet, and Victor had only been the acting boss of the Sontag Clan for a few hours. The feds didn't even know about it, or Valerie would have mentioned it in our little meeting. Victor's accession wasn't the typical mob promotion, and it was going to take time for the rest of the clan to learn what happened and fall in line behind him. It's not like there's a newsletter or an email chain. It would take a few days for him to organize and meet with his managers and set whatever plans he had in motion. In that window was chaos, a day or two when everyone was on a different page. If I was going to take Victor out, it had to be soon. But I still had to find him, and that meant another conversation with Porter.

Victor couldn't have pulled off his coup without Porter's help, and if Porter was involved, he might be able to lead me to Victor. I didn't like thinking about it, but I had to keep in mind another reality. There was a chance I couldn't get to Victor, and I needed to have a backup plan, a way to protect myself if I failed.

Porter was going to give me that insurance policy; he just didn't know it yet.

26

BEGGING AND EGGS

OVER THE LAST FEW HOURS, I'd witnessed Nicky Sontag's assassination, been shot through the leg, watched Joseph Sontag bludgeon his attorney's head with a chair, and been threatened by the FBI. But for some reason, all I wanted to do was eat eggs and pancakes. I also needed to talk to Zoe, but she wasn't going to be happy with what I had to say.

I parked in front of Dalt's Diner, a few blocks down from Hoster Hall, and rang Zoe. I asked her to meet me at the diner and she agreed. While I waited for her, I ordered a water, two eggs over medium, bacon, and a short stack of Georgia pecan pancakes. Ten minutes later, Zoe walked into the diner and sat down beside me, waving off the waiter before he made it to the table to take her order.

"What do you want now?" She stared at me through her mirrored sunglasses.

"I need a loan. A pretty big one."

"Why?"

"It's a long story, but I need to get Spiro and Napoli off my back."

"How did you get into debt with them? Figured you were smarter than that."

"I was standing next to Nicky Sontag when Spiro and Napoli had him killed. I need to throw some cash at them so they don't send anyone after me."

She snatched a piece of bacon from my plate. "And how much is that going to cost you?"

I swallowed hard. "I figure two million?"

"You've got to be fucking kidding me!"

The old couple behind our booth turned to look at us.

"What makes you think I'm going to give you two million dollars?"

"Not give. It's a loan. And I only need one million from you."

"Only one million?" She shook her head and cupped her hand over her mouth. "Fuck me."

"I'm good for it. You know me."

"Who are you shaking down for the rest?"

"Don't worry about that. Can you help me or not?"

She hesitated.

"Zoe, I don't have a lot of options here."

"It seems like I'm your only option. For everything. Ever since you came back here, all you've done is take shit from me." She smacked my cell phone across the table, sending it into the metal napkin dispenser. "You're even using my goddamn cell phone!"

Two other families turned to watch us.

"I'm beginning to think you're a bad investment, Connor. You're not paying off."

"I'll get you the money back, plus interest. This is the last thing I'll ask from you."

"I doubt that." She crossed her arms. "You know, we used to have a symbiotic relationship; I help you, you help me, and everything is cream and caramels. But now you're more like a parasite. You just take, and take, and take."

"I'm good for the money, Zoe."

"You're in way deeper than the million. You're also paying me for the club. If you hadn't come back, it would still be standing. You're covering the renovation, plus interest."

"So you're loaning me the money?"

"I'll loan you the money, Connor, but you need to listen very carefully." She took off her sunglasses and leaned over the table so we were face-to-face. I had seen Zoe's eyes before, but never this close up. They were gray with a tinge of olive green. They were bloodshot, but only on the right side. She looked tired and alert at the same time. I couldn't look away, and after a few seconds it was uncomfortable. I blinked hard and refocused on her face.

"Don't misinterpret my kindness for weakness. You'll pay me back everything you owe me, or I'm going to do some terrible things to you, and then I'm going to fold you up and put you someplace they'll never find you. Do you understand?"

"Got it. How quickly can you get the cash?"

"Pick it up tomorrow morning. Nine o'clock. Back of my club. What's left of it."

"Thank you."

She drilled her index finger into my chest. "And this is the last favor I do for you, understand? Don't ask me for anything else. Anything."

"I won't."

She stood up. Her eyes retreated back behind her mirrored

sunglasses and she left the diner, walking faster than she'd come in.

AFTER FINISHING MY MEAL, I returned to my Jeep to make a call. Three people wanted me dead, at least three that I knew about. The only thing that was going to stop Victor was the bullet I planned to put in him. That left Alfred Spiro and Armand Napoli. Witnessing a mob assassination isn't good for anyone's health and they were likely relying on Victor to punch my ticket, but I wasn't going to let that happen. I needed to make sure they weren't going to call up someone else to do it, someone I might not be looking over my shoulder for.

Spiro wasn't difficult to find. He operated out of a restaurant on the west side of the city. It took a few phone calls, but I finally got through to someone who connected me to Spiro.

"What do you want?" said Spiro.

"I'm on my way out of New York, and I've got a deal for you and Armand."

"Go ahead."

"Two million to let me walk away. And I keep my mouth shut about what I saw at The Gramercy Park Hotel. One million each."

He thought for a moment.

"You got that much cash?

"Yes, I do."

He thought again.

"I'll clean your slate, kid, but I can't speak for Armand. You'll have to broker that deal yourself."

"He's my next call."

"Victor owns your contract," said Spiro. "You can buy your

way out from under me, but he's another story. And I don't think he's gonna let you walk. For any price."

"I'll deal with Victor, but you and I, we're good?"

"We're good as soon as I get that money."

"I'll set up the drop after I talk to Armand."

"Make it happen, then." He hung up.

Organized crime runs on two things, fear and money. You'll go far if you've got both, but one will do in most situations. I've seen people buy their way out of mob contracts all the time. It's not something most people know about, but it's there. And it's a lucrative practice.

I needed to give Zoe enough time to organize the million dollars before I set up the drop with Spiro. Finding Victor and Nash was my next priority.

27

GOING ON THE RECORD

VICTOR TAN WAS COMMITTED to seeing me dead. At least, he should be. I was the only outsider who was present for Nicky's death at the Gramercy Park Hotel, and that alone should secure my death warrant. Victor had me at a disadvantage when it came to resources. He had more trigger fingers than I did, and I'd wager a few of those resources were focused solely on bringing me down. While he might have me beat in sheer numbers, he had a weakness I could exploit. He had an operation to run, which meant his ability to keep a low profile was limited. He had to meet with his men, schedule sit-downs, and get Sontag's operation, now *his* operation, back on track.

I had the upper hand in one aspect though. I could outmaneuver him. I could go under, disappear for any length of time I wanted, locate him, wait him out, and then strike whenever it suited. I was like a shark. As long as I was underwater, I had the advantage. But as soon as I surfaced, I'd lose the element of surprise and risk taking a harpoon to the gills.

I didn't plan on surfacing too often, but I had to come up to see Porter. He was the only person who might have information on where to find Victor and Nash, and my survival depended on getting to them before they got to me. Stepping out in the open was a risk I was willing to take.

I didn't know if Victor's crew would be staking out Porter's club, but it made sense to enter through the back door, just in case.

Porter's wine bar opened in about an hour, but his white Jag was already sitting in his private spot. I drove around the block, parked, and walked to the back door.

The sign next to the entrance read KORK KITCHEN DELIVERIES ONLY. I knocked on the door. A moment later, a young man wearing a suit opened the door. I knocked him to the side and moved through the kitchen. The kitchen staff didn't notice me; they moved about focused on getting the place ready for the first customers of the night.

It didn't take me long to navigate the back of the house and make it to the iron spiral staircase that led to Porter's private office. I took the steps two at a time until I reached the top, where one of Porter's bodyguards grabbed me. He wrapped me in a bear hug, twirled around and flung me into the wall. A second man appeared, this one brandishing a 9mm Beretta.

"I'm here to see Porter," I said.

"No shit," said the one with the weapon. He nodded to the other. "Call him."

The bald man in the suit pulled a cell phone from his inside pocket and dialed. "You've got a guest." He looked at me.

"Connor Harding," I said.

"Connor Harding," the man repeated. Porter said something and the man with the phone grimaced, as if pissed that he wasn't going to get to kill right then and there.

"Arms against the wall," he said.

I did as he told me. He searched me and dropped my .45 and cell phone on the table at the top of the stairs. "Go on. You've got five minutes."

Convinced I wasn't going to be any trouble, the man with the 9mm returned the weapon to the shoulder holster under his jacket. Sensing my chance, I tucked my chin against my breastbone and exploded into him, striking his nose with the top of my head. The cartilage crunched. I withdrew and repositioned to attack him again. He stumbled backward, and blinded by the blood pouring into his eyes from his shattered nose, he collided with the other bodyguard and they both fell down the spiral staircase.

I grabbed my phone and weapon from the table and charged Porter's office. I kicked the door with so much force that it flung open, bounced off the doorstop, and snapped closed after I'd stepped in.

Porter jumped to his feet behind his desk as I leveled the .45 at his chest.

"Call them off, or I'll Norman Bates ya right here."

A moment later the door opened again, but Porter waved his men off before they crossed the threshold. He told them to take a walk, and I listened as their heavy frames lumbered back down the hall.

"What in the hell is this all about?"

"It's about you working with Victor Tan to overthrow Sontag, killing Nicky, and more importantly, coming after me."

I slipped one hand in my pocket and kept the one with the gun pointed squarely at Porter.

"You're only part right, Connor."

"Enlighten me."

He breathed deep and sat on the corner of his desk, his

hands folded in his lap. "Listen, after Sontag got picked up, Victor came to me and said if it looked like Sontag was going to go away for good, then he wanted a chance to talk to Nicky about taking over. I told him to hold off. Sontag has beat this shit before, and I thought he could beat it again. But they didn't grant him bail, and with him inside, Spiro and Napoli were getting anxious. Victor came to me again wanting to know my intentions. I told him to cool off and wait it out, to see what happened with Sontag. It was obvious he wasn't getting out, and they were going to take their time going to trial. Sontag was going to be off the street for a long time, maybe permanently.

"Victor approached me a third time and said he was getting word from his men one of Spiro's crews was moving into our territory, just to poke us a bit and see how we'd react. I heard the same from my men. The other clans sensed weakness with Sontag out of the picture and no clear successor. We had to do something to hold them off."

"What about Nicky?"

"I don't care who runs things. I liked Nicky; never had a problem with him. If it were up to me, I'd gladly fall in line behind him, but the rest of the clan didn't have faith in him. Sontag was a killer and he commanded respect. Nicky didn't have that. He was a joke and was in over his head. Even if Sontag did want him at the top, the rest of the men weren't going to go for it. And with Sontag in prison, what's he going to do about it?"

"So you encouraged Victor to take Nicky out?"

"No. Victor came to me and said he was going to talk to Nicky to get his buyout. Victor thought with his father looking at life in prison, Nicky might want to walk away."

"You didn't sanction the hit on him?"

"How could I? I wasn't in a position to sanction anything. I simply told Victor that I wouldn't stand in his way and that I wasn't going to make a play for the top spot myself. That I'd back him when the dust settled."

I was quiet.

"Look around you, Connor. You know as good as I do the only way to survive all this is to walk away. While you can still walk. I'm on my way out. I've got a five-year plan. Five more years of this shit and I'm out. I don't care who takes over for Sontag, as long as it doesn't affect my operation here."

"Why did Victor come after me?"

"I have no idea."

"I find that hard to believe. You seem to know everything else about Victor's plan."

"I've always been honest with you, Connor, and I'm not bullshitting you when I say I had nothing to do with the hit on you or Nicky. That didn't come from me, and had I known about it, I would have stopped it. It's reckless and unnecessary."

"Reckless and unnecessary? You mean like snatching an FBI agent off the street and torturing him for information?"

"That's different."

"How so?"

"Sontag and I both thought someone on the inside was working against him. Messner said he was getting paranoid sitting in that cell. The only thing he had to think about was who turned against him. I wanted to know too, because they could still be in the organization, feeding the feds information on all of us. Trying to take us all down. Then I got a call from one of my men who had a contact inside NYPD. He gave me the name of an agent who was part of the organized crime task force. I paid him a visit and got him to tell me all about his source inside the organization."

"And the agent, he fingered Messner?"

"No. He fingered you. That agent gave you up in less than a minute. I kept torturing him, convinced he had more than one informant, but nope. Just you."

"If you knew it was me, why did you give up Messner?"

"Because I didn't want to give you up."

"Sontag crushed Messner's skull with a chair. Right in front of me."

"Better him than you."

"Why?"

"Because I never liked that slimy son of a bitch, and because Messner knew enough to put us all away. So that should convince you that I had nothing to do with the hit on you. If I wanted you dead, I would have told Sontag the truth and they would have wheeled you out of MCC on a gurney, not Messner."

"Why not kill us both then? Why let me live knowing I talked to the feds?"

"I wasn't ready to give you up yet. Maybe I thought there was still some use for you around here. Don't look a gift horse in the mouth."

I didn't say anything.

"I explained myself," said Porter. "Now it's your turn. Why are you working with the FBI and what did you tell them?"

"I'm not working with them." The .45 was getting heavy in my hand. "They approached me years ago looking for information. I told them to fuck off, but they threatened to put my father away. I didn't have a choice."

"What did you tell them? And who did you implicate?"

"I didn't implicate anyone. I convinced them I only did odd jobs for Sontag. I gave them an idea of how he worked, what businesses he was in, and who was in his organization. Most of that, they already knew. They just needed confirmation. I intentionally kept things vague, just enough to keep them interested, but not enough to affect anything here."

"That's a fine line to walk."

"Yes, it is. I'm no rat, but I also wasn't about to watch my father get yanked into prison for whatever years he has left."

No one likes a snitch in this business, and I didn't realize why Porter had spared me until he mentioned he might have use for me. Now it was clear. He was going to hang this over my head just like the FBI held my father's possible incarceration over me. Porter would use it for leverage. Do what he says, or he tells everyone I cooperated with the feds. Then every criminal in the city would want me dead. I'd have a contract on my head so big you could see it from space. Normally, I'd consider blowing Porter's head off, but criminal politics are complicated around here. He was still a high-ranking member of the Sontag Clan, and killing him would trigger a chain of events I wasn't yet prepared to deal with.

The trick was to remove his leverage, which is exactly what I planned to do. But, I had another, more urgent issue, so Porter would have to wait. I had to deal with Victor Tan and Eddie Nash, and while I wasn't willing to go to war over Declan Porter, I was willing to do it for them.

"Where can I find Victor?"

"He splits his time between a place in Greenwich Village— 215 Mercer Street, apartment 7B—and Gretchen's bed at The Plaza. You find Victor and Nash won't be too far behind." He smiled wide. "Better hurry though. You'll want to find him before he finds you."

"I plan to."

I left Porter's office. At the end of the hall, one of Porter's bodyguards was sitting in a chair with an icepack on his face. The other was blotting up blood from the floor. I ordered both men onto the floor and then disappeared down the spiral staircase and out the back door. On my way to my Jeep, I pulled Zoe's cell phone from my pocket, closed the voice recorder app, and emailed the file to three different email addresses.

28

215 MERCER STREET

CRIMINALS TEND to stay up late and sleep in the next day. That's why federal agencies usually apprehend high-value targets in the morning. They're still in bed, unaware of what's happening and less likely to put up a fight. This was one of the reasons I decided to move on Victor the next morning. The other reason was I was dead tired, and I wanted my wits about me when I arrived at 215 Mercer Street.

Up until now, my investigation was like setting up dominoes. Slow and methodical. Now it was time to knock them down. I mentioned earlier that offing Porter in his office would put a neon bullseye on my back. I didn't have the authority to go after Victor any more than I did Porter, but in NYC crime circles, I was justified. Victor had issued an unsanctioned hit on me and payback was allowed. I was also counting on Sontag still having enough clout to protect me from inside his cell.

On Friday morning, I parked two blocks away from Victor's Greenwich apartment. A doorman was standing in front of the building. He wore tan slacks, a gray sweater and a camel, cashmere overcoat. A trendier look than the old-fashioned red and gold uniforms. He opened the door as I approached and I motioned him to follow me in. He did.

"Can I help you?" he asked.

"You've got a fugitive in apartment 7B and I'm here to bring him in." I flashed a pair of handcuffs that I kept in my glovebox.

"Mr. Tan?"

"That's right."

"You law enforcement?"

"No. I'm a skip tracer. Mr. Tan jumped a $250,000 bond." I held up an empty white envelope. "I have arrest authority through Midtown Bail Bonds."

"You're a bounty hunter?"

"Skip tracer, but yes." I returned the envelope to my inside jacket pocket before he had a chance to ask for it.

I was surprised he knew a skip tracer and bounty hunter were the same things. Most people don't, but I was betting he didn't know the legal limitations of what a skip tracer can and can't do. Those details are often overshadowed by the romanticized depictions of bounty hunters. Even if I was legit, the doorman had no legal obligation to let me into Victor's apartment. Had I been the real deal, I would have brought a uniformed police officer with me. He would have the authority to enter the premises, and I'd take the bail jumper into custody and return him to lockup. Of course, none of that was going to happen, because none of this was real.

In my experience, no one cares about the law in situations like this. I was hoping the doorman, and the property manager, if the doorman decided to call him, was more concerned that they had a fugitive at their luxury apartment complex than whatever legal right I had to apprehend him.

The bet paid off, because the man in the camel overcoat escorted me to the elevator, removed a key card from his pocket, and scanned it on a black square sensor.

"Is he violent?" he asked.

The elevator door opened and I stepped on.

"No. He's standing trial for financial crimes. I wouldn't worry about it. I doubt he's even here, but I need to check his residence, just in case."

The doorman was still nodding his head when the door closed.

I didn't ask him for a master key because I already knew he didn't have one. The manager could probably get one, but that would take too long, and there was no guarantee he'd let me in anyway. Better to take my chances with a doorman who was less likely to ask many questions.

The elevator door opened on the seventh floor and I walked to apartment 7B. Placing my ear next to the door, I listened for a television, conversation, or any other sign someone might be behind the dark-gray door. Nothing, but that didn't mean Victor wasn't home.

I screwed the suppressor onto my .45 and opened the door with my own master key—a size twelve work boot strategically placed an inch above and to the left of the keyhole. The lock tore through the jamb, sending shards of pine across the apartment's foyer. I moved through the apartment with military precision, scanning the room down the sight of my weapon. Nothing. I completed my initial search and returned to the foyer, where I closed the door the best I could with a broken frame, before more thoroughly turning the place over.

Across from the foyer, in the living room, was a white sofa and a flagstone coffee table. I checked the pile of mail on the table. The postmarks on the unopened envelopes told me Victor hadn't touched his mail in a few days. The beds were still made and there were vacuum marks visible on the area rugs throughout the apartment. I moved to the kitchen, where I found a large white calendar attached to the side of the refrigerator with a gray, hooked magnet. There was a reminder written on every Tuesday this month. MANHATTAN MAIDS. It had been three days since they'd cleaned his apartment, and by the looks of the vacuum tracks and mail, Victor hadn't been back since.

I slipped into the bedroom. There was a small modern-looking desk in the corner. Above the desk, a window overlooked a yoga studio. I rummaged through the desk drawers in hopes of finding anything that might point me in Victor's direction, but there was nothing. I opened the bedroom closet door and found two coats, three suits, and a few other articles of clothing. I checked the coat pockets. One of them turned up nothing. The other contained a key card for The Plaza Hotel, likely for Gretchen's room.

Aside from the clothing and mail, there was no other evidence anyone was living here. Perhaps Victor preferred to take up residence with a sultry redhead in a luxury hotel. I was about to find out. I pocketed the key card.

Before leaving, I plucked a black permanent marker from the desk, walked into the living room and wrote in large letters on the white sofa.

I'M COMING FOR YOU, VICTOR.

I pocketed my weapon and rode the elevator back to the

lobby, where the doorman ran up to me with an eager look on his face.

"What ya find?"

"No dice. He's gone and I don't suspect he'll be back anytime soon."

"Got any other leads?"

I almost laughed at the question, but assumed this was the most excitement a doorman in Greenwich Village had experienced in a long time.

"Just one." I thanked him for his help and returned to my car.

GRETHEN'S HOTEL room was my next target, but first I had to make a withdrawal.

Zoe wasn't at Hoster Hall, or at least that's what her man told me when I arrived at the back of her club. I peered through the rear door as he loaded a duffle bag into the back of my Jeep. The inside of Hoster Hall was a charred jumble of exposed studs, dangling wires, torn insulation, and flaking paint. The place smelled more like a wet dog than a tinder box.

The man shut my lift gate. "Zoe asked me to remind you of the terms," he said.

"Pay her back or she's going to murder me."

"That's about right."

I thanked him and drove to The Plaza Hotel.

29

THE CRIMSON CON

THE PLAZA HOTEL maintenance crew was decorating the lobby for the holidays. They had constructed a large iron frame and were filling it with potted poinsettia plants to make a giant, red, leafy Christmas tree.

I had Victor's key card in my pocket, but without knowing which room Gretchen was in, it wasn't going to be much help. If this were a low-end hotel, it would be easy to convince the front desk jockey to drop me her room number. My go-to play was to tell the clerk I was there to give a massage to a guest, and while I had a name, I didn't have a room number. That's worked before, but it wouldn't work at The Plaza. No masseur heading to The Plaza Hotel would be dressed like me, and more importantly, the staff here would be trained to protect guest privacy. HR likely had produced a video course on it. Top shelf VIPs stay here, and they value their privacy. I wouldn't get past the front desk, so I wasn't going to try.

Instead, I simply asked the thin man with the fake tan to ring Gretchen Sontag's room. I counted the rings on the other end. He hung up after seven and asked if I wanted to leave her a message. I told him I didn't and then took a seat in the lobby, away from the front door, but still in view the entrance.

Gretchen walked into the lobby an hour and a half later carrying shopping bags from Bergdorf Goodman and Burberry. She walked passed the front desk to the elevator bank. I followed, and when the door opened, I stepped in behind her. She didn't notice me until she turned around and reached for the panel of numbers.

"What floor?" I asked.

"Connor, what are you—"

"I said what floor?"

"Ten."

I pressed the number and opened my coat to show her the .45.

"What are you doing?"

"You're going to open your hotel room door, and if Victor Tan is there, I'm going to put a bullet through his head."

"Why would Victor be in my room?"

"Cut the bullshit."

The elevator dinged and the door opened to the tenth floor. I moved to her side and wrapped my left arm around her, pulling Gretchen close to me—one happy, cozy couple. My right thumb rested on my belt buckle, inches away from my weapon. As we walked down the hall, the Burberry bag bounced off my left thigh. We didn't pass anyone.

She stopped at room 1012.

"You scream or warn him, and I'll kill you too, Gretchen. It won't be a thing for me, and I think you know that."

She nodded and set her bags down so she could get the key card from her purse. I stepped behind her, checked the hallway, and pulled the .45 out of my coat. When the door was open, I pushed her through the entrance, where she tumbled to the floor. I kicked the door closed behind us and stepped over her, my weapon raised. Her room was small. Only a bedroom and bathroom. A suit laid across the side of the bed. I moved to the bathroom and peered in, but it was empty. Victor wasn't here.

I pointed to the suit. "Where the fuck is he, Gretchen?"

"I don't know."

"Is he coming back here?"

"I said I don't know." She struggled to her feet, wobbling on her black stilettos. I grabbed her arm and flung her onto the bed.

"Damnit, Gretch—"

"I don't know!" She was crying. "I don't know where he is or where he's going."

I pointed my weapon at her. "You set me up."

She put her hands in front of her face. "I had nothing to do with it."

"Did you know they were coming to Boston?"

"I didn't know it was you."

"So you did know about it? What Victor was doing."

"I knew he was trying to edge Joseph and everyone else out. He said he was sending Eddie to Boston, but I didn't know it had anything to do with you. I didn't even know where you were."

She lowered her hands to reveal her running eyeliner.

"But you told him I was here. When I came to the city."

"Yes, I told him. He would've found out eventually."

The .45 grew heavier in my hand, but I kept it raised. I wasn't going to shoot Gretchen, because even with a suppressor on my weapon, it would still be loud enough for anyone in the adjacent rooms to hear it. Making it Hollywood-quiet meant lubing the suppressor with oil or water, something I didn't have time to do. Gretchen didn't know my intentions, and staring down the barrel of any weapon has a bowel-emptying effect.

"You told him I was here and he followed me. Followed me all the way to Nicky's place."

"I told him you were in the city because I knew if you found out who was behind the Boston thing, you'd kill Victor."

"I am going to kill him. Eddie Nash too."

"What about me?"

"What about you?"

"They'll kill me. I don't know who, but someone will. Porter, I don't know."

"Maybe you should just wait and see who rises to the top and then start sleeping with him. You're good at that. Maybe it'll save your ass for a while."

I picked up the Plaza-branded pen and notepad from the desk next to the door and tossed them on the bed.

"Make a list of all the places Victor could be."

"I don't—"

I stepped forward, placed the weapon against her forehead, and nudged her back into the ornate gray and bronze head-board. "Make the goddamn list."

She started to hyperventilate as if going into shock, so I eased off.

"Now," I said.

She struggled to click open the pen, her hands shaking. I lowered the .45 and placed it back inside my jacket. She wasn't going to be able to concentrate otherwise. Just as I slid it into its holster, the cell phone in my pocket buzzed. I answered and held it to my ear.

"You get my money?" said Zoe.

"Picked it up earlier."

"I meant, did you pay it back yet?"

"You'll get it." I pressed the receiver tight to my ear so Gretchen couldn't hear the conversation. "I'm a bit busy right now, can you bust my balls about this later?"

"You can count on that. I want to keep it top of mind for you."

"It's tip-top."

"That's not the only reason I called. One of my associates just spotted Eddie Nash walking into Molly's Pub on twenty-second and third. Want to go kill him?"

"Too public."

"We have to get there before he leaves or we'll lose him."

I thought back to Nicky's assassination. "I'll call you in five minutes. Don't do anything."

I knew where Eddie was going, but I didn't want to say anything that might tip Gretchen off. A phone call would get to Victor and Eddie much faster than I could.

"Five minutes," I repeated and hung up the phone.

Gretchen handed me a list of three hotels. She was still shaking.

"He usually stays at these places. I don't know if he's there or not, but those are the only ones I can think of."

I folded the paper and slipped it into my pocket.

"Victor and Eddie are going to die and there's nothing you can do to save either of them." I took her cell phone from her purse and smashed it beneath my boot. "If I find out you tried to warn them, I'll add you to the list too."

She nodded.

"Things are going to get bad real quick, Gretch. You might want to think about disappearing for a while."

I left her crying on the bed.

I WAS BACK on the phone with Zoe before I left the lobby of the hotel.

"Eddie Nash is staying at the Gramercy Park Hotel," I said. "I can be there in twenty minutes. Meet me there."

"Make it quick. If I see him, I can't promise he'll be alive when you get here."

"Don't do anything without me. Nash might be the only way I can find Victor. Just hold tight."

I pulled onto Lexington Avenue and did everything I could not to hit a red light or yellow cab. I don't know why I hadn't made the connection earlier, but when Eddie and I exchanged shots at the Gramercy Park Hotel, there was a metal suitcase on the bed. It made sense someone was already staying in that room when they set up the meeting with Nicky. Gretchen's list of Victor's haunts didn't include the Gramercy, so it made more sense that the suitcase belonged to Eddie. It's wasn't a certainty, but Eddie being in that neighborhood, and the suitcase I saw yesterday, were strong enough leads to check it out. Had anyone else been staying in that room, the police would have cleared them out after a shootout, but Spiro and Napoli were both there at the time of the shootout, and they had enough juice with the NYPD to get them to look the other way.

Zoe was leaning against her car, a suitcase at her feet when I arrived. She grabbed her case and we were in the hotel lobby a minute later.

"Did you see him come back?" I said.

"No. And it took everything I had not to go into Molly's and blow the shit out of him right then and there. He burned my place down and he's going to pay for that."

"I won't fight you on that, but I need to know where Victor is first. Then you can do whatever the hell you want with him."

"What's the plan?" she asked.

"He's staying in room 722. Take the elevator up to seven and wait there. I'll have the front desk call his room. I'll tell them I've got a delivery for him and make sure he didn't switch rooms. If he answers the phone, we'll know he's in there and we'll storm it together. If he doesn't answer, then we figure out another way to get in, so we're there waiting when he comes back."

"I got nothing better," she said, wheeling her suitcase into the elevator.

I gave her a few minutes to reach the seventh floor, then I stepped to the front desk. My eye followed the desk clerk's hand as he dialed Eddie's room. He was still in 722. They rang him, but he didn't answer. I thanked the clerk, and after he turned away, I called Zoe to tell her Eddie was still out and that I'd meet her in a minute.

The elevator opened and I blew past a maid pushing a cleaning cart, turned the corner, and arrived at Eddie's room, but Zoe was nowhere in sight.

I waited for a moment, before Eddie's hotel room door opened and Zoe waved me in.

"How did you get in here?"

"The maid let me in. Told her I was here to surprise my husband who was on a business trip."

"And that worked?"

"We're inside aren't we?"

I went to the bedroom, the same room where I'd leaped from the balcony, to find the metal suitcase still there. It was on the floor now. Inside were two handguns, various articles of clothing and a notepad. I thumbed through the notepad, where I found my home address in Boston.

"He's still here," I yelled to Zoe, who was in the main room.

She wheeled her suitcase into the bedroom, unzipped it, and removed a machine gun that looked like something out of a video game. It was heavily modified, with a suppressor and an extra large magazine the size of my forearm.

She sat on the bed next to me, the machine gun in her lap.

"Thanks for the tip about Eddie," I said. "I thought you were done doing favors for me."

"I am. This one's for me. By the way, I'm adding two hundred bucks to the half-mil you already owe me."

"Why's that?"

"I had to tip the maid who let me in."

I looked down at the weapon.

"All right."

WE SAT on that bed for at least an hour before hearing the hotel room door open. I stood up and peered through the space by the door hinges.

"Is it him?" whispered Zoe.

I nodded.

"Is he alone?"

I nodded again.

Zoe pushed me out of the way and charged into the main suite with her weapon raised. As she peered down the sight, she pulled the trigger, strafing the room, hitting everything from the sofa to the wall, to the coffee table, to the two chairs where Spiro and Napoli sat earlier. She fired like she had ammunition to spare, not concerned about anyone else she might hit in an adjoining room or hallway.

Each shot was accompanied by a muffled pop. It sounded more like the clicking of a car with a bad starter than a military assault rifle.

I don't think Eddie even saw her before she put a half dozen rounds into his legs, dropping him onto the plush area rug that adorned the center of the room. He looked up to see me, yelled, and grabbed his leaking shins. Zoe stuffed her hand over his mouth to keep him quiet.

"Where's Victor?" I said.

Zoe removed her hand, stepped back, and tossed her rifle onto the sofa.

Eddie drew in a deep breath and squirmed on the floor. He was sweating, and I swore I could hear his heart beating from a few feet away. He screamed again.

Zoe slipped a six-inch blade from inside her maroon leather jacket and placed it against Eddie's neck.

"Scream again, and I'll slice you open," she said.

"Where is Victor?" I repeated

It took him a few seconds to slow his breathing enough talk. "I don't know. I haven't heard from him. Since yesterday."

"Bullshit."

He started rocking back and forth on the carpet.

"I don't know where he is." He bit into his forearm to keep from yelling and was turning white in front of us. "He left after we did Nicky and I haven't seen him since."

Zoe removed the knife from his neck and cut into his right ear.

"You're not telling us what we want to know," she said.

He started to scream again but clenched his teeth to keep it in. "I don't know!" His breathing was deep and labored. He was fading. "He never came back to the hotel." His words were slow and drawn out.

"You call him?" I said.

"Voice mail. I don't know where he is."

Sontag still had some influence, even in custody, so it was possible he got to Victor after learning about the Nicky hit.

"What do you think, Connor?" asked Zoe. "He being straight?"

The blood from Eddie's legs was seeping into the cream shag carpet underneath him.

"I don't think he knows," I said.

"I don't know," repeated Eddie.

"Too bad." Zoe slashed his throat open and walked back into the bedroom.

I watched Eddie Nash bleed out on the carpet in one of the city's most luxurious hotels. Zoe returned a moment later pulling her suitcase, her semiautomatic rifle tucked away inside.

"I got what I wanted," she said. "Sorry you didn't."

"How in the hell am I supposed to find Victor now? Eddie was my best lead."

"He didn't know where he was, Connor. There wasn't anything he could do for you."

"You don't know that." I returned to Eddie's body and searched his pockets until I found his cell phone. Perhaps there was something in there that would help me locate Victor, or maybe he would call when he was ready to come up for air.

My only next step was to start down the list of hotels Gretchen gave me and hope I got lucky. Unfortunately, luck hadn't followed me to New York, and I doubted she'd show up now.

30

PLAN B

It DIDN'T MAKE sense that Eddie hadn't heard from Victor since Nicky's execution. In this line of work, when people stop returning calls or don't show up for something important, it usually means they're dead. According to Porter, Victor had taken all the right steps not to end up that way. He secured approval from Spiro and Napoli before moving on Nicky, so they wouldn't be behind his sudden disappearance. Sontag had a shorter reach in custody, and while he might be able to orchestrate a takedown against Victor eventually, that was going to take some time. The FBI was another possibility. Valerie didn't mention him when we met at FBI headquarters, but she was unlikely to show her hand even if he was being held in the next room.

That left Porter.

I slipped Zoe's loaner cell phone from my pocket and dialed. Porter answered on the third ring.

"Where are you?" he asked.

"I'd rather not say."

Zoe shifted her ear, trying to catch both sides of the conversation.

"Eddie Nash is dead," I said. "But he wasn't able to give me anything on Victor's whereabouts before—"

"I know where he is," said Porter. "I can take you to him. Tell me where you are and I'll send a car."

Less than twenty-four hours ago, I shoved a .45 in Porter's face and knocked around two of his men. Whatever professional courtesy I'd racked up with Porter over the years had evaporated.

"Why don't you just tell me where he is? You sending a car doesn't give me a warm feeling. No offense."

"Then you're in a bit of a jam, because I'm your only way to get to him."

"Where is he?"

"Nope. Tell me where you are and I'll send a car."

Zoe kicked the metal suitcase with the toe of her burgundy stiletto.

"There's an access alley behind the Gramercy Park Hotel. The loading dock."

"Fifteen minutes," he said and hung up.

We walked to the rear of the hotel, next to the commercial trash bin where I had waited for my shuttle to see Dr. Dresden.

"Why here?" asked Zoe.

"Because that trash bin will provide some good cover for you."

"For me?"

"That's right. I figure I'm worth a million to you alive and nothing dead."

Zoe didn't know her duffle was still in the back of my car.

"You forgot the two hundred I slipped the maid."

"Still, you've got a financial interest in keeping me alive. Porter doesn't."

"So what's your plan?"

"When the car gets here, I shove a gun in the driver's face and demand to know where he's supposed to take me. Then I haul his ass out of the vehicle and drive there alone."

"And I'm what? Supposed to hold the driver at gunpoint until you come back?"

"That's right. But more importantly, if the driver isn't alone, and things go south—"

"They're going to go south, Connor. Your plan is shit."

"If they do, you'll be in position behind that trash can with that street sweeper to even the odds."

"It's a shit plan. Let's get out of here and think this through. It'll take some time, but I'll find someone to locate Victor."

"I don't have much more time. There's a net closing in around me, and the longer I stay in New York, the more likely I am to wind up dead or in federal custody. I have to move now."

"I don't like it."

"Noted."

Zoe rolled her suitcase behind the dumpster and started assembling her assault rifle while I removed the suppressor from my .45 so it would fit inside my front jacket pocket. When I finished, I stuffed both hands in my pockets, leaned against the dumpster and waited like a field mouse scanning for hawks.

A black sedan with tinted windows eased into the alley a few minutes later.

"You ready?" I whispered.

"Uh-huh," said Zoe from behind the dumpster. "Hope you are."

The car stopped about fifty feet away from me. The driver parked so that the passenger side of the vehicle was perpendicular to the garbage bin. To get in the driver's face, I had to walk around the car, putting the sedan between Zoe and me. I didn't like it, but I didn't have much choice.

Keeping my hands in my pockets, I walked around the rear of the car to the driver's door. Nitty Ford, Porter's longtime driver, rolled down the window.

"Get in," he said.

"Where are we going?"

He scanned the loading dock. "Get in, Connor."

I was about to repeat myself when I heard gravel crunching behind me. Another vehicle had pulled in. This one was a navy-blue SUV. It rolled to a stop and two men with MP9 submachine guns stepped out of the back and took cover behind the SUV's rear doors. Had they been with the feds, they would already have me on the ground and would be ordering Nitty out of the sedan. Had they been with a rival clan, they would have already opened fire and Nitty and I would be footnotes in New York's criminal history. But they hadn't arrested us nor opened fire, which meant they were Nitty's backup.

While I had never fired one, I'd seen MP9s in the Army, and they were nasty weapons. I looked back at the garbage bin. Zoe's assault rifle didn't have a scope; it wasn't meant for long-range work. If she fired at either of the men near the SUV, she'd likely miss. She'd also reveal her position and they'd cut her to shreds. And there I was standing directly in the crossfire.

Zoe was right. The plan was shit.

The rear door of Nitty's sedan opened and a man stepped

out gripping a double-barreled shotgun. Before I had a chance to recognize him, he slammed the shotgun butt into the side of my head, dropping me to the ground.

WHEN I CAME TO, I was leaning against the rear passenger window staring at the highway blowing by. My hands were still in my pockets, but my .45 was gone. So was my cell phone. I sat up and rubbed the side of my head.

"Sorry mate," said the man next to me with the shotgun.

Nitty watched me in the rearview mirror.

"Are you taking me to Porter."

"That's right."

"Is he going to kill me?"

"No idea."

My brain throbbed and my right arm was tingling— possible concussion. I looked out the rear window to see the navy-blue SUV trailing us. The man next to me sat against the other door, the shotgun trained on me.

I leaned back against the window. The cold glass eased my headache. From the mile marker we passed, I knew we were traveling north on I-95. Even with my cloudy head, our desti- nation was clear—Sontag's beach house.

I must have blacked out again, because the next thing I knew Nitty was opening the rear car door and catching me as I nearly fell out onto the paver-stone driveway. He helped me up and motioned me toward the front door. I staggered ahead, concentrating on my feet to see if I was walking in a straight line. I wasn't.

The front door was unlocked. I didn't have to turn around to know the double-barreled shotgun was still aimed at me.

Once in the house, I walked down the main hallway toward the back. Porter's bodyguards, the two men I'd jumped at the club, stood in the hall flanking the dining room. One of them rubbed his closed fist, waiting for the order to wreck me.

It's not often you get to march down the same hallway to your probable death twice. The last time Porter and I were in this house, I was reflecting on my life, convinced I was going to die. This time was different because I knew something Porter didn't. Regardless of what he thought was going to happen, I wasn't going to die today.

I stepped into the dining room, where I saw Victor Tan on his knees in front of the long walnut table.

Porter leaned against the back wall.

"Look who I found," he said.

Victor teetered on his knees, his hands tied behind him.

"What am I doing here?" I said.

"You came to New York to find the person who tried to kill you. Here he is."

"You planning on killing us both?"

"No. I brought you here so you could finally get what you came to New York for."

Nitty Ford walked into the dining room and handed Porter my .45. Porter pulled the slide back, checked for a round in the chamber, and then ejected the magazine. He gave the weapon to me with one shot.

"You brought me here to kill Victor?"

"That's right. And to discuss your future."

I thought back to Porter's explanation about Victor asking him to stand down while he orchestrated a takeover of the Sontag Clan. Porter said he agreed because he knew he'd be a liability if he opposed him. But that was all bullshit. He wasn't standing down; he was just delaying his own promotion. He'd let Victor execute his plan, remove all of those soldiers still loyal to Sontag, clear a path to the throne, and then Porter would step in, off Victor and take what he wanted all along. There was just one part that wasn't obvious to me.

"What about Spiro and Napoli?" I asked.

"What about 'em?"

"Aren't they going to be pissed you took out the horse they backed?"

"Victor was never their frontrunner. When Victor first came to me and pitched his plan, I went to Spiro and Napoli and pitched mine. They never backed him. They backed me. So, no. They're going to be just fine with all this. In fact, they're expecting it. Now, go ahead."

I shook my head and handed the .45 back to Porter. "Kill him yourself. I'm not your triggerman."

"You came for revenge. Go ahead and take it."

"I did come for revenge, but you're not going to play me the way you did Victor. If you want him dead, do it yourself."

Porter grabbed the weapon from my hand. He placed it to the back of Victor's head and fired. The slug exited the front of Victor's skull and lodged in the baseboard. I stepped back as Victor's body slumped to the side, blood leaking from his head.

"Now, let's talk about you."

"There's nothing to talk about, Porter."

"Sure there is. You handled a lot of shit for Sontag, and now I want you to handle it for me."

"That's not going to happen."

"And why not?"

"Because I liked Sontag. I don't like you."

"I don't think you understand how this works. Remember

back in my office, when you asked me why I didn't give you up to Sontag? About you working for the FBI? It's because I need your talents. I didn't need Messner. That's why I kept you alive. And it's the only reason you're still alive. Understand me?"

"I don't care what you want. I'm not sticking around. I'm done, Porter. I don't work for Sontag, and I don't work for you. I'm going back to Boston. I'm out."

Porter slid the magazine back into my .45, racked the slide, and raised it to my head.

"You're not going anywhere."

"That's where you're wrong."

The man with the shotgun was still standing in the corner. I motioned to him.

"Give Porter my cell phone," I said.

He looked at his boss, waiting for the okay. Porter nodded and the man handed over my cell.

"Check the outgoing text messages," I said. "There's only one there."

Porter fumbled with the cell phone for a moment. "What's this?"

"It's your confession, asshole. I recorded our conversation in your office. The one where you admitted to torturing and killing a federal agent."

Porter tapped the button and we all listened.

"You'll see I sent that message to three email accounts. Don't bother trying to figure out who they went to. They're all encrypted accounts. If anything happens to me today or any other day, that message finds its way to the FBI, and you're done."

Porter stopped the recording.

"You're not the smartest person in the room, Porter. You never were."

Porter looked down at Victor and then to me. "You think you're going to hold this over my head forever?"

"I'm not holding anything over your head. I'm saving my neck. As long as you don't move on me, that recording goes nowhere. You don't have to worry about it."

"What if someone else pops you? I'm sure there's a growing list of people who want to put you in the ground."

"Probably. That's why it's in your best interest to keep me nice and safe. That reminds me. Alfie O'Bannon wants me dead. You're going to want to call him off. He won't like it, but as long as he's part of Sontag's Boston network, he'll abide by it."

"Son of a bitch."

"I have no interest in sending you away. Just to keep breathing. But right now, what I want is to get the hell out of New York." I snatched my .45 and my cell from his hands and stuffed them back in my pocket. "And I want Nitty's keys. I'll leave the car in Gramercy Park."

Porter stood there thinking. He was trying to figure out an option where I didn't walk out of there. Nothing came to mind, because he motioned to Nitty, who tossed his keys my way.

I walked out of the dining room, passing a half dozen men who minutes earlier were all ready to kill me. I opened the front door, climbed into the black sedan and rolled off the driveway with a smile on my face and a massive headache.

Then I dialed my phone.

31

ONE FINAL DEAL

PORTER WOULD NEVER REST KNOWING I had evidence against him. Once he calmed down, he'd realize he only had one option. He'd send someone after me. Then he would torture me the same way he tortured agent Werner. He'd demand to know who had the recording, and if he used his pressure washer, he'd likely get an answer out of me. Then he would kill me.

Mr. Fish and Albert were right. Consequences, they always catch up to you. I had made one final deal that I hoped would get me out of New York alive and guarantee my safety wherever I settled down, at least temporarily. I dialed Spiro.

"I'm on my way out of the city," I said. "I've got your money."

"Bring it by."He started rattling off an address.

"No. We do it in public. Meet me at Grand Central. The Campbell Apartment."

"When?"

"I'm on my way there now. Better hurry before I blow it all on scotch." I hung up.

I stashed Nitty's car at Gramercy Park and exchanged it for my Jeep. I checked that the duffle with Zoe's cash was still in the back. It was.

I parked a block away from Grand Central Terminal, tossed the duffle over my shoulder and headed to the Campbell Apartment. A million dollars isn't as heavy as most people think. Stacked in hundred-dollar bills, it only weighs about twenty-five pounds.

Despite its name, the Campbell Apartment isn't an apartment. It's a bar tucked deep inside the terminal. Close to three-quarters of a million people walk through Grand Central Terminal every day, but only a few lucky souls know this place exists.

I arrived to find an attractive woman in a long coat sitting alone at a table. She was reading a newspaper and enjoying a cocktail. Next to her was a small group of businessmen in suits. A few other tables were occupied too, but half of the others were empty. I ordered a Balvenie Caribbean Cask Scotch from the bar and took a seat at the back of the room.

ALFRED SPIRO ARRIVED before I finished my drink. He had four men with him. Spiro sat on the red sofa across from me. His men remained on their feet. He nudged the duffle with his black wingtip.

"That for me?" he said.

"That's right."

Spiro leaned over, unzipped the duffle and riffled through the stacks of hundred-dollar bills. Satisfied, he leaned back on the sofa.

"You square up with Napoli too?" he said.

"I did."

That was a lie. I never contacted Napoli, but that would have cost me another million, which I wasn't about to ask Zoe for. I only needed to get a meeting with one of them.

"Then I guess we're square."

"One more thing," I said. "Why did you back Porter over Victor?"

"Victor's a hothead. Doesn't think, just acts. He would have created a lot of trouble for everyone. Porter is more stable. Knows how to run things."

"And what about Nicky? Why kill him?"

"Nicky had to go. We didn't need another Sontag at the helm. Porter seemed like the best option."

"So you, Napoli and Victor planned Nicky's death, and then threw Victor under the bus, so Porter could take over the operation?"

"It's a messy business."

"Sure is." I stood up. "I appreciate the deal. I assume we'll never cross paths again."

"Don't see why we would."

I nodded, slipped a hand in my pocket and walked passed Spiro's men toward the exit. The men in suits didn't pay me much attention, but the attractive woman looked my way and smiled.

I tossed her the USB drive from my pocket.

"Hope your transmitter worked," I said. "Check the drive too. Declan Porter had some interesting things to say about your dead FBI agent. It's all on there. Don't know how strong it is, but it'll give you something to work with."

"That's all we need."

The men in suits stood up and walked toward the back of the room as a half dozen more stormed in from the hall.

"There's a million dollars in that duffle back there. I'd like to get it back."

"It'll go into evidence for now, but I'll make sure it gets back to you. Might take a few years."

"I won't count on it."

32

DANGEROUS DEBTS

AND JUST LIKE THAT, everything I'd come to New York to do was done. Victor Tan and Eddie Nash were dead and I'd guaranteed my safety. For a short time anyway.

Zoe Armstrong wasn't kidding when she threatened to kill me over the million I owed her. I intended to get it back to her, but I didn't know how long it would take Valerie to clear it with the bureau. That could take a long time, and I didn't want to leave town without reconfirming my intention to pay her back.

I checked out of Hotel Beacon and drove to Hoster Hall. Someone had posted a red-and-white sign in the front window: CLOSED FOR RENOVATIONS. From the outside, you'd never even know the place had been on fire days earlier.

The door was unlocked and there was a crew of a dozen or so working to clean up the place. The fire had destroyed most of the inside of the club, but the fire suppression systems saved it from being a complete loss. The brick walls were scorched in some areas, but that just added to the club's ambiance. The long bar had been torched and was nearly gone. The main stage had suffered some damage, but it was salvageable.

Zoe's bartender was mopping up puddles of water on the floor. He swayed back and forth, dragging the mop from side to side. The mop handle kept getting caught on the Beretta he wore on his hip. He saw me watching him, raised two fingers to his lips and whistled the way I'd always wanted to learn how to do. Zoe approached as soon as she saw me.

"I'm glad you're not dead," she said. "Now you can pay me back."

She took her sunglasses off her V-neck, white T-shirt and slipped them onto her face.

I opened my wallet and handed her two crisp hundred-dollar bills.

"That leaves a balance of a cool mil," she said. "I don't do payment plans."

"I'll pay you back, Zoe. Just give me some time."

She walked over to where the bar used to be and grabbed a bottle of whiskey from the floor, poured two glasses, and handed one to me.

"Victor?" she said.

"Dead."

"By you?"

"No. Porter."

She nodded. "He running things?"

"For now, although I think it'll be a short stint."

"How's that?"

"The FBI took Alfred Spiro into custody less than an hour ago. Napoli and Porter probably won't be too far behind."

"And you had some role in that?"

"I did."

"Then you just painted an even larger target on your back."

"I'm okay with that. Those three are going to have a lot more to worry about than little old me. And when they do decide to come after me, they won't find me. I'll be a ghost in a few days."

She brushed her long hair away from her face and dove into her glass. About the FBI. I have to ask, Connor."

"No. Your name never came up."

"I'm glad to hear that. You figure they'll be back?"

"The feds? Doubt it. I've given them enough so we can part ways amicably."

"What's your next move?" she said.

"I'm going back to Boston to heal up. I've still got a hole in my leg and a headache the size of your insurance claim. Then I'll vanish."

"Right, mirage man."

"But I'll still pay you back."

"Better work fast. You don't want to be in debt to me, Connor. Because as long as you are, you'll work it off. Sometime soon, I'm going to call you, and you're going to pick up. And then you're going to say yes to whatever I ask you to do. And then you're going to do it."

"I just got out from under the FBI's thumb. Porter's too. I'm not working for anyone anymore. That includes you."

"You're into me for six zeros. I've put people in the ground for much less than that. You're going to work it off."

She stared at me with a look that said the conversation was over. I took the hint and walked to the front door. Then I grabbed Zoe's cell phone from my pocket and tossed it to her.

"Thanks for the loaner."

She threw it back. "Keep it. That way, I know how to get a hold of you."

I opened the door and walked out.

"Connor, drive safe. You're no good to me dead."

On that, we agreed.

33

WISER FOR THE TIME

IT TOOK three and a half hours to make it home from New York City, but it felt a lot longer. The house was dark when I arrived. I entered through the kitchen door and did a thorough sweep of the house before limping upstairs to go to sleep. I hadn't had a good night's sleep in a week, and it was time to end that streak.

I laid the .45 on the nightstand next to me and eased into bed. I blinked once and the numbers on the clock read 11:45. Blinking again, they read 2:15. My eyes snapped open at 3:32 a.m. to the sound of glass breaking. I sprung up, threw the blanket off and grabbed the pistol from the nightstand. I listened for more glass or the sound of the kitchen door opening, but it was quiet.

Moving through my bedroom doorway, I pressed myself against the wall in the hallway and slowly inched down the stairs toward the living room. I stopped and scanned the living room. Nothing. I heard another sound. I couldn't be sure what it was, but it came from the kitchen. I moved against the wall again, focusing in front of me, but scanning the living room to my left periodically in case someone was trying to lure me in one direction only to jump me from another. I made it to the bottom of the steps, and after rechecking the living room, I turned the corner into the kitchen, my .45 raised. I knelt and flipped on the kitchen light.

Nothing.

The room was empty.

I checked the back door, but it was still locked. All of the glass panes were intact and the kitchen windows were closed and locked. I swept the house again, carefully inspecting every door and window, checking every corner and closet twice. The place was clean. Satisfied I was alone, I returned to the living room and sat on the couch. I propped my feet up on the coffee table and set the .45 in my lap. It was still dark, and while I couldn't imagine how anyone could still be in the house, I didn't want to close my eyes. It was nearly four in the morning, and the sun would be up in a few hours. I'd check the house again in the daylight, but until then, I'd sit here and wait.

I moved my fingers up and down the slide of my .45, listening for any sign someone was in the house. Nothing came. Maybe the initial noise was outside. Maybe O'Bannon's men had been casing my place, waiting for me to come back. Or maybe Porter sent a button man to retrieve the recording I made implicating him in agent Werner's murder.

After a few minutes, my leg started throbbing. I'd left a bottle of painkillers on my nightstand, but I wasn't about to move from the couch. I couldn't risk revealing my position.

I slumped down on the couch so my head wasn't visible through the front windows. I'd hear the front door open if someone tried coming in that way, and could rotate off the couch and get a shot off before they even noticed I was there.

If they entered through the back door, I'd see them before they saw me and deliver the same result. Under the circumstances, I could still move quickly, bum leg and all. Either way, I had the advantage.

Once it was light outside, I'd walk the perimeter of the house to look for any signs someone was here. A gum wrapper or a cigarette butt, something to prove I wasn't hearing things.

It was Saturday, and I would have to get Albert from the bus terminal at six o'clock this morning. I had some time to kill. I sat perfectly still for another hour, listening. Nothing. My leg was numb now, so I eased it off the coffee table and winced as the pain intensified. The .45 was still in my lap, and I moved my finger up and down the slide to stay awake, waiting for the sun to rise.

FOLLOW CONNOR HARDING

Connor Harding will return.

Sign up for pre-launch updates and notifications about the next book at www.traceconger.com/freebies.

Can't wait for Connor's next adventure? Check out the Mr. Finn series, featuring Connor's brother, Finn Harding.

A NOTE FROM THE AUTHOR

I've never found writing a novel to be an easy task, but this one was a particularly tough bastard. There were several starts and stops, and the manuscript gathered a lot of dust along the way. There was a two-and-a-half-year span from the time I began writing the first draft until it was published, which for me, seemed like an eternity. Hopefully the final product doesn't reflect those growing pains.

If you enjoyed this novel, please consider leaving an online review at your favorite virtual bookstore or on your social media pages. Reviews from readers like you help me spread the word about my fiction.

If you'd like to learn more about my work, contact me, or sign up for updates and free fiction head over to www.traceconger.com. I'll see you there.

Trace Conger

Cincinnati, Ohio

ACKNOWLEDGMENTS

This novel would not have been possible without the generous support of several individuals. I'd like to personally thank the following people for their direct and indirect involvement in giving this project life:

Andrew Bockhold, Christine Grote, and Jeff Hillard for reading early versions and helping me course correct and my editor, Elizabeth A. White for taking a mess and turning it into less of a mess.

Thank you also to Joe Lansdale, Lawrence Block, and Roger Hobbs for your inspiration.

ABOUT THE AUTHOR

Trace Conger is an award-winning author in the crime, thriller, and suspense genres. He is known for his tight writing style, dark themes, and subtle humor. Trace lives in Cincinnati with his wonderfully supportive family.

Find Trace online at:
    www.traceconger.com
    www.facebook.com/tracecongerauthor
    www.twitter.com/traceconger

ALSO BY TRACE CONGER

The Shadow Broker

Scar Tissue

The Prison Guard's Son

The White Boy

Made in the USA
Columbia, SC
18 January 2025

52051462R00162